Chip Hilton Sports Series
#22

Home Run Feud

Coach Clair Bee

Foreword by Coach Pete Newell
Basketball Hall of Fame Enshrinee

Updated by Randall and Cynthia Bee Farley

**BROADMAN
&HOLMAN
PUBLISHERS**

Nashville, Tennessee

© 2002 by Randall K. and Cynthia Bee Farley
Printed in the United States of America

0-8054-2124-6

Published by Broadman & Holman Publishers,
Nashville, Tennessee

Subject Heading: BASEBALL—FICTION / YOUTH
Library of Congress Card Catalog Number: 2001043007

Library of Congress Cataloging-in-Publication Data

Bee, Clair, 1900–83
    Home run feud / Clair Bee ; updated by Randall and
Cynthia Bee Farley ; foreword by Coach Pete Newell.
        p. cm. — (Chip Hilton sports series ; #22)
    Originally published: New York : Grosset & Dunlap, [1964].
    Summary: Chip sees the morale of his baseball team
threatened by the arrogant behavior of first baseman and heavy
hitter Ben Green.
    ISBN 0-8054-2124-6 (pb)
    [1. Baseball—Fiction. 2. Sportsmanship—Fiction.
3. Universities and colleges—Fiction.] I. Farley, Cynthia Bee,
1952– . II. Farley, Randall K., 1952– . III. Title.

PZ7.B38196 Hm   2002
[Fic]—dc21   2001043007

1 2 3 4 5 6 7 8 9 10 05 04 03 02 01

WESLEY "BO" GILL

"World's Greatest Sports Editor"
Friend and booster of the "Home-Run Kids" and all the
"little guys" who share with him a love of baseball

COACH CLAIR BEE, 1964

EMMANUAL LAMONIER*
AND HIS BOGOR KIDS

RANDY AND CINDY FARLEY, 2002

*Emmanual, a 1996 graduate of Jakarta International School, has returned to
Indonesia after completing his college degree and has opened an orphan-
age for children in Bogor, Indonesia. We honor Emmanual for his love,
devotion, and tremendous courage.

Contents

Foreword

BASKETBALL BEGAN its rise in national interest in the 1930s. The recently formed National Association of Basketball Coaches (NABC) led a policy that would elevate college basketball to a major competitive sports level. One of the leaders of this movement was also the successful coach of the Long Island University Blackbirds, Coach Clair Bee.

Coach Bee was exceptionally popular in New York because of his great success as coach of Long Island University and a tremendous gift he had with people, especially the New York press. Madison Square Garden was the mecca of college basketball with its national schedule of outstanding teams competing in their double header schedule and the National Invitational Tournament (NIT), considered the national championship of that time period.

Clair Bee was a leading figure in initiating this tournament because of his great Long Island University teams and his ability to propel a reluctant press to support the tournament. Clair was a leading figure in the rise of basketball interest that has strongly contributed to the current acceptance of college basketball as one of our leading sport entities. Besides his other great contributions, Clair originated the famous one-three-one zone that is still one of the most effective zone defenses in the game today.

Coach Bee also authored the twenty-four-volume Chip Hilton Sports series that became one of the most popular youth series ever written. Clair was a wonderful, creative, and leading college basketball coach, and I am happy to have been a friend of his.

Coach Pete Newell
Member, Basketball Hall of Fame

CHAPTER 1

Hometown Hero

CHIP HILTON'S spirits were as high and light as the fleecy white clouds floating in the blue spring sky as he strode along the tulip-lined campus sidewalk. Over the tops of the budding elm and maple trees, State's baseball grandstand came into view, and his heart leaped. It wouldn't be long now! The opening game of the State University baseball season was only two days away, the first of a two-day series with State's bitter conference rival, A & M. Since Chip was captain of the team and the number-one pitcher, Coach Henry Rockwell was almost sure to start him in the first game on Friday.

"Hey, Chip, *slow down!* Wait for me," Soapy Smith pleaded, stretching his stocky legs in a determined effort to keep up with his roommate's brisk pace. "We're way early for practice. Besides, you'll need some of that energy Friday. I figure the Rock will make you do some throwing this afternoon too. You know *him.*"

"I know him," Chip said calmly, slowing his pace, "and I hope he does just that."

Soapy peered up at Chip in surprise. "This is Wednesday," he said pointedly, "but the Rock's going to start you Friday for sure. You should take it easy."

"Not this afternoon."

"What's so special about this particular afternoon?" Soapy asked.

"Everything. I've got to find out something."

Soapy's head shot sideways, and he eyed Chip knowingly. "Ben Green! Right?"

"Yep."

"That's what I thought. Is your arm all right?"

Chip studied his battery mate's worried expression for a moment and then grinned. "Never better," he said lightly.

"Then, *this,*" Soapy said, speeding up his steps, "I can't wait to see. But remember," he warned, "not even Ben Green is worth a sore arm. If something happens to that pitching arm of yours, the season is shot."

"Not to worry, Soapy. Nothing will happen," Chip said reassuringly.

"What we need are some first-rate pitchers," Soapy observed seriously. "Even one more would be a big help. Someone sure better turn up before Saturday."

"Dean could do it."

"Sure, if he didn't fall into one of his wild throwing episodes. Dugan and Sparks were all right for high school, but they're just not good enough for Division 1 college ball."

"Everything will work out all right," Chip said slowly. He meant to express confidence, but deep inside he knew it was wishful thinking. Soapy was right. The Saturday pitcher was a question mark at the moment. Something had to be done about State's pitching situation. Eliminating himself, there were only three possible starters. So far, not one of the three had shown himself to be Division 1 caliber.

It didn't seem possible that a team could have so many fine catchers, infielders, and outfielders and only two or three reliable pitchers. Coach Henry Rockwell had tried to make pitchers out of some of the extra players, but not one had shown enough ability or determination. Every other position on the team was staffed with veterans, but that wasn't the half of it. The talented newcomers were challenging the veteran players for starting positions. Chip figured that was good pressure because it kept everybody hustling, but it didn't solve the pitching problem. In truth, the pressure actually contributed to the team's difficulties. The chief obstacle to State University's quest for the conference title and a chance to repeat as national champions was team morale. The team spirit that had been the Statesmen's biggest asset the previous year was gone with last season's championship. Nothing remained except bitterness and tension, and, as far as Chip could see, just one person was the source of all the trouble.

Matching strides, the two lifelong friends continued on toward Alumni Field. Chip could already smell the freshly mown grass of the outfield. As they neared the players' entrance, the crack of a bat meeting the ball and the shouts of players rang out invitingly. With Soapy right on his heels, Chip eagerly quickened his pace and hurried through the gate and down the steps under the grandstand to the State University locker room.

They found the room deserted except for Murph Kelly, State's veteran trainer. "You're late," he announced sourly.

"Sorry, Murph," Chip apologized, hustling over to his locker.

"We had late classes; it's a lab day for both of us," Soapy explained.

"Do you fellows need anything?" the old trainer asked swiftly. "If not, you'd better step on it. It's an important practice game this afternoon. Coach is gonna try to find some ballplayers so he can decide on a starting lineup."

"Find some players?" Soapy echoed. "Are you kidding? He's got more players than the Yankees!"

"I said *ballplayers*," Kelly growled. "I mean kids who appreciate team play and don't try to smack the ball out of the park every time they get hold of a bat. By the way, you're both on team A."

He paused for a moment and then continued pointedly, "In the dugout! Dugan is pitching and Engle is catching for your side, and Dean is working for team B with Nickels doing the receiving."

Picking up his trainer's kit, Murph headed for the field.

Chip and Soapy finished dressing and clattered into the hall and up the runway to the hometeam dugout. Every player in sight was busy. Coach Rockwell was hitting grounders to the infielders, alternating between veterans and new candidates, and Bill Malone, State University's new assistant baseball coach, was fungoing long, high flies to the outfielders.

Chip tossed his glove on the grass in front of the dugout and started his laps. Coach Henry Rockwell believed a pitcher was only as good as his legs and made his pitchers run and run and run some more.

"Hey!" Soapy complained. "You don't have to sprint all the way. This is baseball, not track and field!"

Chip laughed and slowed down until the redhead caught up. "Hey, Soapy, I was just thinking about this baseball story I read. Years ago, some minor-league manager would stop the team bus every fifty miles and make his players pile off the bus and jog a mile down the road before the bus would pick them up again. That's how he kept his players in shape."

Soapy grunted, "Real funny! Whatever you do, don't you *ever* tell Rockwell that story!"

Both laughed even harder, and then Chip picked up the pace again. His thoughts drifted back to his boyhood, and he remembered the work ethic his father had instilled in him: *If an athlete is going to get anything worthwhile out of a workout, he has to put something into it each and every day.*

Finishing a hard sprint, they got their gloves and began to play catch at the warm-up plate. Warming up was always important to Chip. No matter how long it took him to loosen up, he never threw carelessly. Instead, he worked on control and tried to put every pitch in the strike zone. Soapy had been Chip's battery mate ever since they were in high school at Valley Falls, and the freckle-faced redhead knew just what to expect.

Coach Henry "The Rock" Rockwell blasted his whistle, and the B team players hustled in for batting practice. Chip kept throwing until the players began to hit. Then he pulled on his warm-up jacket and signaled Soapy that he was ready. Side by side, they walked past the bat rack and leaned against the fence. There they watched the B team batters take their swings, analyzing, as always, the batting strengths and weaknesses of each player.

The player at bat was Ellis "Belter" Burke. Belter was a returning letterman, and Chip knew all about his likes and dislikes. He was a switch-hitter and could hit equally well from either side of the plate.

Now, facing Terrell "Flash" Sparks's right-hand throws, he was batting lefty. Burke looked over the first pitch and then hit three of the little pitcher's serves squarely against the left-field fence.

Then the veteran outfielder moved to the first-base side of the plate and powdered Sparks's first throw, sending the ball high over the right-field fence.

"He just absolutely ruins the ball," Soapy said in admiration.

"That isn't all," Chip added. "He can lay it down too."

Chip had scarcely finished speaking when Burke bunted a high fastball, sending a slow roller down the third-base path. It was a tough pitch to bunt, and it confirmed Chip's high opinion of the powerful outfielder. Burke dropped his bat and sped down the first-base line, sprinting all the way to the bag.

"Picture play," Soapy exclaimed loud enough for everyone to hear. "S-w-w-e-eet play, Belter!"

Chip nodded, but he wasn't thinking about Burke. He was sizing up the burly hitter with the mouth full of bubble gum who was strutting to the plate. Ben Green stood six-five and weighed 225 pounds. Green had the knack of getting all of his weight into his batting swing. He tried to kill every pitch, attempting to knock the ball over the fence every time he took a swing.

Now, before entering the batter's box, he went through an elaborate warm-up ritual. Holding three bats, he whirled them over his head several times, tossed two of them away, hitched up his pants, stooped to fill his hands with dirt, and then yanked at the brim of his red and blue State batting helmet. Then he stepped up to the third-base side of the plate and got set.

Sparks took his stretch, but before he could throw, Green stepped back out of the box and turned toward Chip. Shifting the bulging lump of bubble gum from one side of his mouth to the other, he lifted his bat and pointed it over third base. "Just for you, I'm gonna park this one over the left-field fence, captain," he called arrogantly.

Chip made no reply. Green had looked in his direction, but the big hitter's eyes had been focused over Chip's head, on a man sitting in the grandstand. A few student fans were sitting under the big shelter, but Chip and every ballplayer on the field had noted the well-dressed stranger. The man was old enough to be a player's grandfather proudly watching his grandson out on the diamond, but his tanned face, keen eyes, and big-boned body spelled baseball, major-league ball. Chip thought the man was Stu Gardner, a veteran scout with the New York organization.

Gardner had talked to him when Chip was in high school about being drafted to play in the Yankees farm system and about what to consider in signing a major-league contract. Chip remembered that the Yankees scout had differed greatly from many of the men who had contacted him. Gardner had advised him to finish college before making a decision.

Chip had liked the man so much that he promised to talk to Gardner about signing with the Yankees as soon as he got his degree. He had received several letters from the scout, but this was the first time he had seen him since his high school days.

Most of the big-league scouts were like Gardner. But the "bird dogs," the small-time talent chasers, were different. They made rash promises and tried all sorts of tricks to ingratiate themselves into a young player's good graces.

One or two had even offered bonus money to Mary Hilton, Chip's widowed mother, at the family home in Valley Falls. After the death of his father in an industrial accident at the Valley Falls Pottery, things had been tough for Chip and his mom. But Mary Hilton's position with the phone company had kept things together. Then, as now, Mary Hilton had wanted her son to have a good education more than anything in the world, and despite the fact that the bonus money would have greatly eased their financial stress, she and Chip had given all of the big-league scouts and sports agents the same answer. Only after Chip had earned his college degree would they decide whether he should try professional baseball.

"Hometown show-off! A real poser!" Soapy growled, bringing Chip's thoughts back to Ben Green. "What's with the pointing to the fence? What's he trying to do, make like Babe Ruth?"

"He hits a long ball," Chip said quietly.

"Sure!" Soapy retorted. "When and *if* he hits it."

"He hit twenty home runs last summer."

"Sure! But how many times did he strike out?" Without waiting for a reply, Soapy added sarcastically, "Huh! Town ball. A dinky local summer league."

Sparks's first throw to Green came in around his knees, and the big batter passed it up. The next pitch was far outside. Green started his swing and reached for the ball. But before his wrists broke, he pulled the bat back. "Come on, Sparks," he called angrily, stepping out of the box, "what are you trying to do, *act* like a pitcher?"

"He crowds the plate," Soapy observed.

"A straight pull hitter," Chip added.

Green glanced quickly toward each dugout before planting his feet in the front of the batter's box. Swinging his bat in a circle around his head, he twisted his spikes firmly into the clay. He pounded the plate with his war club. Then, with a darting glance over his shoulder toward the man in the grandstand, he poised his bat, buried his chin in his left shoulder, and focused his eyes intently on the pitcher. Sparks waited until Green was set and then dealt a fastball around the batter's knees. Green put everything he had into a vicious swing, but his bat cut under the ball and he fouled it back against the screen.

"Wrong direction, Ben," someone called.

"Try hitting backward," another added.

"Put some of that bubble gum on the bat," another cried.

Green disregarded the barbs and remained in the batter's box. But he did flap his elbows and pull the bat through in several vicious cuts while he waited for Sparks to throw.

The pitch came in high and fast, and Green took a full cut. There was a sharp crack and the ball took off for the left-field fence. Chip followed the flight of the ball with his eyes for a moment but knew it was in there, a homer all the way.

A group of young middle school boys had been roaming beyond the heavy steel fence, waiting hopefully for home-run clouts. They saw this one coming and took off in a head-long dash before the ball cleared the barrier. Chip chuckled. The State University Athletic Department wasn't going to get *that* ball back.

The force of his swing pivoted Green clear around, and he nearly fell to the ground. The bat saved him. He jabbed it in the ground. Chewing away on his bubble gum, he grinned once more in Chip's direction. "Far enough for ya, captain?" he cried.

Chip nodded. "A home run in any ballpark."

"Good!" Green hollered. "Now I'll drop one over the *right-*field fence."

"Oh, brother, give me a break," Soapy managed.

Some of the A team players greeted Green's announcement with hoots and jeers, but Chip noted that the power hitters were quiet. Too quiet! As much as he disliked Green's attitude, Chip had to concede that the bombastic clouter had leadership qualities. Several of the veteran long-ball hitters had been following Green's example and concentrating on home runs.

"Attaboy, slugger!" Darrin Nickels yelled from the B team dugout.

"Way to call your shots, Ben. You're the man," newcomer Ricky "Rusty" Gates chortled.

Some of the players who had defended team play now struck back. They had been special targets for the first baseman's sarcastic barbs, and this was their opportunity to get even.

"Hold the trademark up, Green!"

"Watch the water bucket!"

"Just a hometown slugger, that's what he is!"

"No, that's Babe Ruth the Second!"

"Yeah, Ben. Point your bat at the fence!"

Ben Green took the ribbing in stride. "All you guys are just jealous," he retorted, grinning cockily. "Just sit back and watch the master at work."

The big hitter continued to return the taunts and catcalls with good-humored jibes, but Chip remembered the workouts when there had been no one in the stands and felt sure Stu Gardner's presence had a lot to do with Green's joviality. With the famous scout in the stands, it appeared Ben could take criticism as well as dish it out.

University was Green's hometown, and he had starred for the high school team. The previous summer he had batted in the cleanup spot for the local town team. Now he was a candidate for State University's first-base job and was trying to beat out Biggie Cohen, one of Chip's hometown friends. Today the Rock was playing Green at first base on the B team. Like Biggie, he would be hitting in the cleanup slot in the batting order.

Eyeing Green, Chip began to massage the shoulder of his throwing arm. He might not have an opportunity to pitch to Ben Green today, but if Coach Rockwell *did* call on him, he was going all out. His arm was warm and loose, and he had brought it along carefully during the past month. Now he was ready! He was ready for A & M on Friday and more than ready—anytime—for the hometown hero.

CHAPTER 2

Glory and Home Runs

THE BOASTFUL first baseman backed away from the plate and went through his lengthy batting ritual despite a scattering of jeers. He knocked nonexistent dirt out of his spikes, took off his batting helmet, twisted it back on his head, and waggled the bat. Then he dug in at the plate and got set. Chip noted the exaggerated preliminaries, but he was more interested in the first baseman's hitting style.

As Soapy had said, Green crowded the plate. He stood well forward in the six-foot-by-four-foot batter's box to cut down the strike zone. Chip couldn't help wondering how Ben would react to an inside fastball. Good pitching dictated keeping a long-ball hitter off balance.

He got an idea on the very next pitch. From behind the pitching screen, Sparks stretched and came in with a close throw just under Green's elbows. The busy hitter jumped back and glowered at the slender pitcher. "Come on, Flash," he barked irritably, "throw where you're looking!"

"He doesn't seem to like 'em tight," Soapy remarked.

"We'll remember that," Chip said grimly.

The next pitch split the plate knee-high, and Green lashed at it with all his might. But he got only a piece of the ball, fouling it back on the screen. Chip and Soapy exchanged glances.

Green adjusted his pants, once again tapped his spikes with the bat, and glanced covertly toward the grandstand. Then he moved to the extreme back of the box and closed his stance until he was almost facing the A team dugout. Sparks waited for Green to dig in and then whipped the ball across the middle of the plate, shoulder-high.

Ben Green pulled his bat through in a full swing, and the ball sailed high in the air. Chip followed the flight of the ball and grinned whimsically when the youngsters lit out for the right-field fence. He well remembered his own sandlot days; a regulation baseball was a treasured possession.

Green's swing had pivoted him around again, and this time he landed on the ground. He clambered to one knee and, grinning widely, peered at Chip. "Did I call it, captain?" he cried sarcastically.

Chip watched the ball clear the fence. "You sure did, Ben," he called, nodding his head.

Scrambling to his feet, Green turned and tossed his bat toward the visitors' dugout and jogged toward first base. "Did you see those two sail over the fence?" he called loudly to his teammates. Without waiting for a reply, he jerked a thumb over his shoulder. "I sure wish Captain Hilton was pitching this afternoon."

Soapy couldn't take it. He shuffled his feet impatiently and moved closer to Chip. "He's impossible," he gritted through set teeth.

"I know," Chip said softly.

He turned and glanced casually down into the dugout, wondering whether or not the coaches had been listening. Coach Rockwell and Bill Malone were checking batting orders with Bobby Traymore, the team's student manager.

Apparently they were unaware of the byplay. Chip breathed a sigh of relief and turned to watch the next hitter.

"Lucky jerk," Soapy fumed.

"It wasn't luck," Chip said softly. "He *said* he was going to do it."

"But it was an outside pitch and right across the letters."

"That's got nothing to do with it."

"Sure it does!" Soapy persisted. "It was made to order for a right-field poke, for a righty hitter."

"It takes power to knock *any* kind of a pitch over the fence."

Soapy grunted disdainfully. "Huh! Anyone can clobber practice pitches." He thumped his fist hard into his catcher's mitt. "I'd like to clobber *him*," he continued darkly. "He's trouble and keeps shooting off his mouth about how Coach Rockwell doesn't give him a chance to play first base."

"Doesn't give him a chance?"

"That's right," Soapy confirmed.

"But Biggie was the team's starting first baseman all of last year. It's up to Green to prove *he's* the best player for the position."

"That'll be the day! Green can't field and he can't run."

"You don't have to be fast when you can knock the ball out of the park."

"Aw, Chip, he's a sucker for low, inside pitches, and you know it. Good pitchers would read him right off the bat."

"Well," Chip agreed reluctantly, "they might."

Soapy hooked a thumb toward the grandstand. "And a big-league scout would too," he persisted.

"There's no doubt about that."

"He's no good," Soapy continued. "He doesn't care anything about the team. All he cares about is personal glory and home runs. To make it worse, he's got a lot of good guys on the team feeling the same way. All the solid hitters are trying to be home-run sluggers. They're all trying to copy him."

Chip thought back through the past few weeks. From the first day of spring practice, Ben Green had focused the brunt of his bantering barbs in his direction. The newcomer had started out cautiously, studying Chip's reactions. Then, when Chip had shown no resentment, the big first baseman had stepped up the pace and had gone far beyond good-natured team joking and jousting.

Chip had given up trying to figure out Green's purpose. And, despite his friends' anger when the quips became too personal, he had talked them out of retaliation. He preferred to handle Ben Green in his own way.

"I think he's a psycho," Soapy said abruptly, breaking into Chip's thoughts.

"Come off it, Soapy," Chip said, laughing at his pal's prognosis.

"I mean it, Chip. Something's got to be wrong with a guy who chews bubble gum all the time."

"Lots of people chew gum!"

"I still say he's a psycho. Professor Gill was talking about people like him just last week in psych class. Dr. Gill said when certain types of people feel insecure or frustrated, they often make verbal attacks on the very people they admire."

"It's a funny way to show their admiration," Chip murmured.

"Dr. Gill said there was a constant struggle going on in such a person's mind—a struggle between the conscious and the subconscious. The conscious represents the person's desire to be something he isn't, and his subconscious is trying to get him to be himself. I think Green's that way. I don't think he's the sort of guy he pretends to be at all. In my opinion, he's a big bluff. A real phony."

"Maybe so. It seems like he's just trying too hard to fit in with the team."

"Well," Soapy said with foreboding, "he'd better not try any attacks directly on Biggie."

"What makes you think he will?"

"Because that's all he talks about. Except for when he's bragging about himself. He's always saying Biggie is one of Rock's pets. If Biggie hears that, he and Green are going to tangle and Mr. Loudmouth Green is gonna get his head knocked off."

"Soapy, are you trying to say that subconsciously, Green really admires Biggie?"

"That's right. In the same way, I think Green is jealous of you yet still admires you too."

Chip looked toward the grass in front of the third-base bleachers. Biggie was playing catch with Speed Morris and Red Schwartz. Soapy, Biggie, Speed, Red, and he were childhood friends and had played sports together at Valley Falls High before coming to State. Henry Rockwell had been their high school mentor and had joined the State coaching staff the year they entered the university.

He thought back to the previous year when he and his four buddies had won starting berths on the varsity baseball team. It had been a great year all around, for the team and for Chip Hilton. State University had won the NCAA championship, and Chip had been elected captain of the team at the end of the season. If the Rock could develop only a couple of pitchers, the big dream of winning two national championships in a row might be more than a fantasy.

Red Schwartz made a bad throw just then, and Biggie skipped swiftly to his right, trapped the ball, pivoted with lightning speed, and made an underhand throw to Morris. It was a perfect example of Biggie's dexterity. He was fast on his feet and had quick hands and an iron arm. Green had to be out of his mind to think he was a better first baseman than Biggie Cohen.

Chip shifted his eyes back to Green. The first baseman made a big target, and his arm was strong. Green was undoubtedly powerful, but he wasn't in Biggie's class when it came to fielding the first-base position. And, Chip mused,

Green had no conception of Biggie's speed and sheer brute strength.

The bell clanged, signaling the end of warm-ups. Chip walked slowly to the dugout and sat down beside Bobby Traymore. The manager had called out the lineup of the B team players when they took their hitting practice. Now he was waiting to call out the A team batting order.

Soapy was warming up Edwin "Doogie" Dugan to give Al Engle a chance to take his turn in the A team batting practice. On the other side of the diamond, Darrin Nickels was taking Rodney "Diz" Dean's warm-up throws. Chip concentrated on the tall lefty's pitching motion. Dean had all the tools necessary to make a good pitcher except the two most important. He couldn't control his pitches or his emotions.

The A team players were ready at last. Traymore called off the names in order: "Crowell, Morris, Finley, Cohen, Schwartz, Gillen, Durley, Engle, and Dugan."

Crowell had been swinging two bats. Now he walked swiftly out to the plate. The little leadoff hitter played second base as if he had invented it. Ozzie "The Whiz" Crowell was an enthusiastic team player, and he could hit. Batting right-handed, he laced out three Texas leaguers and ran out a perfectly placed bunt.

"He's great!" Traymore said in admiration.

Chip nodded his agreement and watched as Robert "Speed" Morris got set at the plate. Speed was perfect for the push-along spot. He was a master at bunting as well as hitting behind the runner. In the field he displayed the strong arm so vital in making the long throws from the deep shortstop hole, and he was lightning around the bases. Speed batted from the third-base side of the plate, but he could match almost anyone in getting down to first. The speedster pushed three sharp hits into right field and then chased a slow-rolling bunt to first base.

"Now we'll have some fun," Traymore chuckled. "The fence busters are on the scene."

"That's what I'm afraid of," Chip said tersely.

"They won't put many over the fence," Traymore whispered, grinning widely. "After Green hit those two out of the park, Coach Rockwell sent a bag of last year's balls out to Sparks. Every one of those balls is old and has had the life knocked out of them."

Chip grinned and nodded his head. Coach Rockwell had seen Green's show and the effect it was having on some of the other players, and he was quietly going to put an end to it. The Rock was some coach!

Fireball Finley had wide, sloping shoulders and powerful arms. He had lots of speed, he could throw, and he played the center-field position like a Joe DiMaggio or Mickey Mantle. He laid into the ball three times. Each of his blows carried to the outfield, but not one reached the fence. Examining his bat and shaking his head, Fireball went back to the dugout.

Biggie Cohen was up next. He was a natural for the cleanup spot and had the power to break up any game with his long, towering blasts. He was a flawless fielder and could tear the glove off a fielder's hand when he made a hard peg.

Chip involuntarily rubbed the palm of his left hand. Biggie was the only ballplayer he shied away from when it came to playing catch and burning in the throws. He watched Biggie lay into the ball three times with all his might. Each hit had plenty of length, but all were far short of Biggie's usual over-the-fence specialty. He, too, examined his bat on the walk back to the bat rack.

Traymore was having a great time. "See what I mean?" he whispered delightedly.

Red Schwartz was up next. Red lacked the speed of his outfield teammates, but he was a first-class clutch hitter. He got hold of the ball three times and ran out a bunt.

Murphy Gillen batted sixth. Murphy was fast. He had a good arm and played right field like a big-leaguer. Batting righty, he always tried for the home-run blow. He hit the dead balls with everything he had, but they were far short of the fence. Gillen didn't understand it. He hefted his bat and then pounded it on the ground before placing it in the bat rack in the dugout.

Andre Durley liked his hot-corner spot at third base. He could fire clothesline strikes to first base, and nothing he could reach was too hot to handle. Andre was a place hitter and showed his skill now by sending a clean Texas leaguer to each field.

Al Engle, batting in the eighth position, walked out for his hits. Engle was Soapy's chief catching rival. He was two inches shorter than the redhead but twenty pounds heavier. Al's extra weight was noticeable in the power of his swing. The two receivers were about equal in throwing and fielding, but Soapy was faster and smarter. The redhead was a genius at reading batters and spotting their weaknesses. Engle cracked a trio of fly balls. Chip turned to watch Dugan warm up.

Doogie Dugan stood five-nine and weighed about 160 pounds. The little pitcher lacked speed and power, but he had deceptive curves and change-up pitches. Dugan was inconsistent, but he could do a good job when he was sharp. When he was "on," he produced a good pitching performance.

Rockwell, Malone, and the three blue-clad umpires were talking in front of the grandstand. Chip saw the baseball scout slip out of his seat in the grandstand and walk down to the wire screen. He joined in the conversation, and it was obvious that everyone in the gathering knew him. Chip had a better look at the man and was sure he was Stu Gardner.

The warning bell clanged, and the umpires moved out on the field. Coach Malone walked briskly to the visitors' side of the diamond, and Coach Rockwell joined the A team starters in front of the dugout. "All right, men," he said, "the usual ground rules are in effect. Let's go! Lots of pep!"

The players ran out on the field. Soapy took charge of home-plate chores while Engle busily strapped on his catching gear. When Engle was ready, Soapy snapped a final peg to the keystone sack. Crowell gloved an imaginary runner, pivoted, and whipped the ball to the hot corner. Durley took the throw and rolled the ball into the dugout as Engle, adjusting his catcher's helmet, joined Dugan in front of the mound.

The plate umpire dusted off the plate and faced the grandstand. "Dugan pitching. Engle catching," he bellowed. "Play ball!" It seemed a little ridiculous for an intrasquad game, but Rock demanded the real thing from the umpires when they worked his practices.

Soapy trotted back to the dugout and dropped heavily down on the bench. Chip glanced inquisitively at the redhead, and Soapy shook his head. "He hasn't got a thing," he whispered.

The chatter came rolling in from the infielders.

"No hitter, Doog!"

"Get him out of there!"

"All mine, Doogie, all mine!"

From out in center field, Fireball Finley's voice boomed in with his old familiar, "Hey, hey, hey there, Doog, old boy! Hey there!"

Engle squatted behind the plate and gave the sign, and Dugan toed the rubber. He took a full stretch and came in with a curve. It whirled around Davis's knees. The second baseman caught it with the meat of his bat. The ball shot over Durley's head and sped toward the left-field corner.

Schwartz made a beautiful play. Running at full speed, he scooped up the ball with his bare hand and pegged a lightning throw to second base. But Davis slid under Crowell's glove to beat the peg by an eyelash. Jim Foster walked, Jerry Gold flied out, and that brought up Ben Green.

CHAPTER 3

The Grand-Slam Kid

BEN GREEN put on his usual show before stepping up to the plate, and Chip could see that Doogie Dugan was upset by the first baseman's actions. Dugan tried a slow curve, and Green clobbered the ball, putting it far over the left-field fence. But the ball curved foul.

Chip breathed a sigh of relief. That had been close.

The next pitch was just below Green's knees and he passed it up. But the umpire called it a strike. Green's head shot around, and he glowered angrily at the umpire for a long, tense moment. Then, with an obvious effort at controlling his temper, he turned away and pounded the plate with his bat.

Dugan was now way ahead of Green and tried to get Ben to go for a bad pitch. But Green waited him out until the count reached two balls and two strikes. Dugan's next pitch was in the dirt and got away from the catcher, Al Engle. Both runners advanced; Davis reached third, and Foster pulled up at second before Engle could recover the ball. That brought the count to three and two, and Rockwell flashed a sign to Engle. Al promptly called for a time-out and walked to the mound to talk to Dugan.

Chip leaned back and thought over the situation on the field. He figured the strategy would be to put Green on first base, setting up a force play at any base as well as the possibility of getting a double play. Dugan was shaking his head stubbornly as Engle laid out that very plan, and Chip could see that the little hurler wanted to pitch to Green.

Dugan toed the pitcher's rubber and fired his slider, but the pitch lacked speed and seemed to hang in the air just as it reached the plate. Green's bat met the ball squarely; the ball soared high into the air, went spinning out toward right field, and fell lazily behind the fence.

Soapy grunted in disgust and muttered something under his breath. Chip felt the same way, but there wasn't anything he or anyone else could do. It was a beautiful three-run homer. The A team players kept up their chatter as Belter Burke dropped the rosin bag in the on-deck circle and walked up to the batter's box. Chip knew it was taking a lot of trying on the A team's part to be so upbeat.

Burke, hitting lefty, took a full cut at Dugan's first pitch. His bat met the ball solidly, and it sailed over the right-field fence and smack into the center of the ball-chasing kids. Although Chip appreciated their gleeful shouts, their celebration was scant compensation for what was happening to his squad on the field.

Mike Donovan scooted down the first-base line as his hit bounded high in the air in front of home plate. Engle's throw to Cohen was a step late, and Mike was safe at first. Gates and Nickels tried to keep the home-run barrage going, but both were too eager and instead lifted high flies that were easily caught in the shallow part of the outfield. That retired the side, and the A team players came charging into the dugout determined to get those four runs back in the bottom half of the first inning.

They did it, too, with Dean's help. The big lefty was wild and walked Crowell and Morris with eight straight throws. Before Fireball Finley had a chance to step up to the plate, Coach Bill Malone came out of the dugout and called time. He talked to Dean for a few moments and then went back to the dugout.

The pep talk didn't help much. Dean got the ball over for a called strike and then threw three straight balls. With the count at three and one, Finley put the wood to a high fastball and drove it all the way to the center-field fence. The blow scored Crowell and Morris, but Mike Donovan played the rebound perfectly. He pegged the ball to the plate and held Fireball to a three-bagger.

Finley didn't stay perched on third very long. Biggie Cohen, batting lefty, looked at two bad throws and then blasted the third pitch over the right-field fence. Once again, the yelps of the youngsters came riding in as they chased the ball. They were having a field day.

Schwartz walked. Gillen hit a hard grounder to Gold and was safe at first when the diminutive third baseman fumbled the ball. Schwartz held up at second. Andre Durley then smashed a sharp line drive directly into Foster's glove. The shortstop pegged the ball to second base and doubled-up Schwartz, who couldn't get back to the bag in time. Gillen was the sole base runner with two outs until Engle worked Dean to a full count before gaining a free pass to first base. Team A's scoring attempts were abruptly halted when Dugan struck out on three straight pitches to retire the side.

Team B scored four more runs in the top of the second inning, but team A had to be content with two tallies in its half of the frame. At the end of two innings, team B was out in front 8-6.

When team A took the field at the top of the third, Rockwell left his place near the dugout steps and sat down between Chip and Soapy. "You two feel like working a few innings?" he asked.

"*Do* we!" Chip exclaimed, picking up his glove. "Watch our smoke."

Soapy grabbed his catcher's mitt, and they hustled out in front of the third-base bleachers to warm up. Before Chip had a chance to make a throw, he heard Green's sarcastic yelp of delight.

"Hey, guys. Looky there! Look over there, guys. Fresh pitcher meat!"

Chip ignored Green and concentrated on his warm-up throws. But he knew what was happening on the field. Dugan had lost his control and couldn't find the plate. He had walked Dean, Davis, and Foster to load the bases when Rockwell called time. Walking out on the diamond, he talked briefly to Dugan and then waved Chip toward the mound and Soapy behind the plate.

Green really got on Chip then, but his barbs didn't register. Chip was trying to assemble his knowledge of Jerry Gold's ability with the bat. He knew Green was in the on-deck circle swinging several bats and that Belter Burke was standing in front of the bat rack, but Gold was the immediate problem. He would take them one at a time.

Chip got the feel of the mound and fired his warm-up pitches to Soapy, thinking about Jerry Gold with every throw. The stocky third baseman was a good hitter who carefully looked over each incoming throw and made the pitcher bring the ball in there. Chip intended to do just that. He wasn't going to walk in any runs!

Gold was only five feet, six inches tall, which he used to his best advantage at bat. His short stature reduced the size of the strike zone, and Jerry abbreviated it even further by using a crouching stance. Chip checked the runners and saw that Speed and Crowell had moved up to the baselines, set for a play at the plate. He sized up Gold again and decided to keep his pitches high. Then Soapy gave the sign and Chip grinned. The redhead seemed to be able to read his mind.

Checking the runners once more, he paused a second and then burned the ball in for a called strike. Then he came back with a low outside curveball that was wide of the plate. With the count one and one, he fired another fastball. Gold fouled back to the screen and out of play.

He was ahead of Jerry now and figured the third baseman would expect him to waste a pitch. Soapy wanted an outside curve, but Chip shook him off until he got the sign for a slider. He took his stretch and put all the speed he could command on the pitch. The ball headed for the outside corner and then blazed back toward Gold, letter-high. Jerry didn't even swing; he stood stock still in his tracks with a bewildered expression on his face as the ball blazed past him and smacked into Soapy's glove.

"Strike three!"

Green had been swinging three bats in the on-deck circle. He tossed two of them away. Then, changing his mind, he called, "Time!" Stalking back to the rack, he tried several bats until he found one that suited him. During all these unnecessary preliminaries, Chip turned his back and played catch with Durley. He didn't see Green swagger up to the plate and put on his usual show, but the catcalls of his teammates gave him an inkling of the ever-present performance.

"Play ball!" called the umpire.

Chip waited behind the pitching rubber until Green stepped into the batter's box. Soapy flashed the sign for a fastball. Chip stepped forward and toed the rubber as Green eyed him cynically. Chip studied Ben Green's cocky, artificial grin for a moment as a burning fire of anger suddenly blazed in his heart. *Keep it cool,* he said to himself. *You have no right to be so angry when obviously this guy has some problems.* But he wanted to strike Green out, even if he never pitched another game as long as he lived.

Jim Foster, on first, had edged a step away from the bag, and Chip suddenly whirled and fired the ball to Biggie. It was a good throw, and Biggie made a perfect tag. But the base umpire spread his hands to his sides in the safe sign. Biggie walked slowly toward the mound.

"Nice throw, Chipper," Biggie commented, tossing the ball to him.

He watched Foster until Biggie returned to the sack, but his thoughts were on Green. He meant to keep ahead of the braggart all the way!

When Chip faced home plate, he saw Green had moved to the front of the box, his legs spread wide, bat held high, and elbows well extended. Chip checked Soapy's sign and then toed the rubber. Taking his stretch, he lowered the ball to the hold position and waited the full second. Focusing his eyes on Soapy's target, he fired the ball toward the inside of the plate. Green lifted his bat in the air and leaped back just as the ball dipped under his elbows and caught the inside corner.

"Stee-rike!" the umpired bellowed.

Then the burly hitter really put on an act. Still holding the bat over his head, he reared back on his heels, his mouth agape. He stared in disbelief at the umpire. Then, shaking the bat menacingly, he took a long stride toward the arbiter. "Whaddaya mean?" he bellowed. "He brushed me off! The ball missed the plate by a foot."

The umpire gazed stonily at Green for a second. Without saying a word, he pulled a whisk broom out of his hip pocket and brushed off the plate. Walking back to his position behind a grinning Soapy, he turned and impassively called, "Play ball!"

Green glared sullenly at the umpire and then spat on his hands. Stepping back into the box, he thumped his bat angrily on the plate and glowered at Chip. "You got away with that one, Hilton," he snarled.

Soapy had kept the ball. He held it up in front of Green. "Came in pretty fast, didn't it?" he asked, chuckling. "You sure you weren't scared?"

"Don't swallow your bubble gum, Ben," someone yelled from the stands.

There was a roar of laughter from both sides of the field, and Green backed out of the box and looked at the umpire. "Well," he asked sarcastically, "are we gonna play ball or fool around?" The umpire ignored him. Green waited until Soapy fired the ball back to Chip and then stepped into the batter's box.

Chip noticed that Green had moved back so he was standing even with the plate, and he felt a glow of satisfaction. The gabby guy was leery of the close ones.

Standing behind the rubber, he waited for Soapy's sign. The redhead called for another inside pitch, but Chip shook his head until he got the sign for a curveball. Before he could toe the rubber, Green stepped back out of the box and again called for time.

This time Green apparently had something in his eyes. Dramatically dropping his bat, the first baseman wiped away at each of his eyes, glaring at Chip each time. Chip was sure Green was faking, but he waited patiently. At last Green picked up his bat and stepped into the box.

Chip faked a throw to Durley to drive Dean back to third and then stepped up on the rubber. This time he took a full stretch, lowered his hands, and then remained in the hold position while he checked Dean. Chip aimed the ball straight for Soapy's glove and sent it whistling in with all the spin he could muster. The ball broke across the inside corner of the plate around Green's wrists and thumped into Soapy's glove as Green's bat swished through in a vicious swing. Strike two!

"He's swingin' like a rusty gate, Chipper," Soapy shouted, whipping the ball back.

Soapy called for a waste pitch, and Chip grinned again. The redhead sure was thinking. He was maneuvering for the setup pitch. Chip blazed the ball toward the outside corner, beyond reach of the big player's bat.

One ball, two strikes!

Green had taken a half step toward the ball and then backed out of the box. Looking first at Chip and then at the umpire, he shook his head in resignation. Chip's teammates really got on Green then.

"Your feet get wet, gabby?"

"Step up and take your medicine, slugger."

"There's a dust-off pitch coming up, bubbles. Better duck!"

Green glared at Chip for a second and then stepped back into the box. Chip noted that Ben had skipped his usual batting ritual and decided the needling was getting to the big guy.

Now Chip was ready for the payoff pitch. Soapy called for the slider, and Chip nodded in agreement. He stepped up to the rubber, checked Dean on third, looked back at Davis on second, and then blazed the ball with all his might toward the outside corner of the plate. The pitch must have looked far outside to the determined batter. At any rate, he waited too long. Green stood with his bat held high and watched helplessly as the ball broke toward him and darted knee-high across the inside corner of the plate.

Soapy dug the ball out of his glove, held it out at arm's length, and regarded it fondly. Then he kissed the ball and pegged it back to Chip. Two away!

Green stood motionless for a long second after the umpire had called, "Strike!" Then he whirled and threw his bat savagely toward the bat rack. Boiling with anger, he stalked toward the dugout. He was razzed loudly from the field.

"Can't hit 'em if you can't see 'em, bubbles."

"Those home runs you got last summer—were they in the softball league?"

For a moment Chip felt a twinge of remorse, even a feeling of sympathy for Green. Then he remembered all the times Green had badgered him and he set his jaw. Green hadn't seen *anything* yet.

Standing behind the mound, Chip watched Belter Burke toss away the warm-up bat and pick up his favorite war club. Belter was a dangerous switch-hitter and would bat lefty against Chip's right-handed pitching. Belter stepped into the box and tapped the plate with his bat, a picture of relaxed confidence.

Soapy squatted in front of the umpire and gave the sign for a curveball, tapping the inside part of his left leg. Chip nodded. A pitch to the inside part of the plate might force Burke to move back a little and unbalance him. He toed the rubber and pulled the string on his curve.

What followed was so lightning fast that he didn't realize what happened. There was a sharp crack, and then a blur of white shot straight at his head. The second crack seemed like an echo until he felt the pain in the palm of his left hand. Chip looked in astonishment at the ball he was clutching in his glove. Instinct and good pitching form had saved him; he had caught the speeding liner on the fly. He heard the shouts of his teammates and realized he was walking toward the dugout with the ball still held tightly in his glove. His glove hand felt as if he'd been playing catch with Biggie Cohen, but the inning was over!

Chattering a mile a minute, Soapy pried the ball away from him and rolled it out to the mound. The fielders came running in with excited celebration to pat him on the back. Biggie broke it up gleefully, calling, "Come on, you guys! Let's go get us some runs."

Chip huddled down in the dugout and studied the B team lineup. Diz Dean was pitching and Darrin Nickels was behind the plate. Ben Green was at first, Pat Davis at second, Jerry Gold at third, and Jim Foster at short. With the exception of Green, the entire infield was made up of sophomores. Belter Burke, Mike Donovan, and Ricky Gates were in the outfield spots.

Crowell and Morris worked Dean for walks to lead off the inning. Finley stepped up to the plate with runners on first and second. Dean fired a blazing fastball for a called strike. Fireball fouled off the next pitch and passed up a curve that missed the strike zone to bring the count to one ball and two strikes. Finley was trying to kill the ball and topped the next pitch for an easy groundout from Davis to Green.

Biggie was slugging, too, and his screaming line drive a few feet inside the third baseline tore off Jerry Gold's glove as he dove for the ball. Jerry quickly recovered the ball in time to hold Ozzie Crowell at third base. Speed stood on second as Biggie occupied first. That brought up Red Schwartz to loaded bases and only one out. As chants of "Rally time!" and "Ducks on the pond!" rang from the dugout, team A withered away its best opportunities to score as Red and Murphy Gillen both swung for the fences and came up empty.

Chip nearly duplicated his one-two-three pattern in the top of the fourth. Mike Donovan reached first base on a fielding error by Crowell, but Chip struck out the next three batters.

In the bottom of the inning, Durley led off and singled to left field. Soapy swaggered up to the plate as Chip walked out to the on-deck circle with a warm-up bat and his favorite stick. The hit-and-run was on, but Soapy blasted the ball hard, too hard. Durley had been off and running, and when Gates nabbed the line drive and pegged the ball to first for the attempted double play, Durley barely made it back. There was one on and one out when Chip tossed the warm-up bat away and moved to the plate.

"Here comes the all-American, Diz," Green cried enthusiastically. "The grand-slam kid himself!"

CHAPTER 4

The Welfare of the Team

THE ANGER came flooding back. Chip tried not to let it show, tried not to let Green get under his skin. Coach Rockwell was in the third-base coaching box and flashed the sign to hit away. Chip was on his own. He took a practice swing and concentrated on Dean.

"He can't hit the size of his hat, Diz," Green yelled menacingly.

Chip took a deep breath and forced away the urge to knock the ball over the fence, but when the pitch came in, he took a mighty swing. The swing missed the ball by a foot.

Green's obnoxious jeers snapped Chip out of a daze. He backed out of the box, giving himself time to focus his concentration as a batter. It didn't help. He did the same thing all over again on the very next pitch, going for a wide, breaking curveball he couldn't have reached with a broom. He felt the hot blood of embarrassment surging under his skin and again stepped away from the plate. Ben Green, the first baseman, had him on the run.

"Knock that cover off the ball, captain," Green taunted. "Go on, slugger, show up the other hitters. Be a home-run pitcher!"

The digs hurt. He waited a moment to cool off and gain his composure. Chip stepped up to the plate in control of himself and determined to look them over, concentrate solely on the ball, and try to meet it. It was time to forget about busting the fence.

Dean powered the next pitch right across the middle of the plate. Chip should have met it right on the nose, but he held back. He tried too hard to regain his timing, and the result was a weak tapped roller straight up the alley. Dean fielded the ball, saw there was no play on Durley speeding down to second, and leisurely threw Chip out at first by twenty feet.

Green took the throw and held the ball until Chip crossed the bag and turned to come back. The big first baseman held the ball out toward him. "Here, Hilton—captain," he said, "take a look at that home-run ball you missed. Stick to pitching, youngster. Leave the hitting to the men."

Back in the dugout, Chip berated himself furiously. He had let Ben Green's bench jockeying get under his skin and earned just what he deserved. *It won't happen again!* he fumed silently.

The next up was Crowell, who walked. Speed hit a hard grounder to Foster and was safe at first when the sophomore shortstop fumbled the ball and wisely decided not to try a forced throw to first base. Crowell held up at second, and Durley danced on third. Finley hit a hard fly to Belter Burke's right, and the left fielder grabbed it on the dead run for the third out, with three team A men stranded on the bases.

Chip was still furious with himself when he left the dugout for the mound in the top of the fifth. If he hadn't let Green get his goat, his team could have easily been out in front instead of two runs behind.

The top of team B's batting order was up, with Davis leading off. Chip couldn't concentrate, and the second baseman worked him for a walk. Foster advanced to the plate, and Chip gave himself another pep talk. This had gone far enough.

He signaled to the umpire for time and then took a long stretch, closing his eyes as he did so and trying to clear his head. *Help me to relax and take my time,* he prayed silently. *I need to let go of this right now and do my job. I need to ignore Green and his taunting and just play the game.*

Pitching carefully, he got Foster on a curve for a strike. His fastball was a hair outside. Then, with the count one and one, Foster fooled him and laid down an almost perfect bunt just beyond Soapy's reach.

Chip swooped down on the ball, prepared to try for the almost impossible cutoff throw to second base. Soapy's frantic yell stopped him. "First base, Chip! First base!"

Digging the ball out of the dirt, he whirled and made the throw to Biggie, but the split second he had hesitated was enough for Foster to beat the peg by a step. The play had advanced Davis to second, and Gold was up. He didn't waste any pitches on the third baseman but fired three fastballs past Gold and struck him out for the second time.

One away!

Now Ben Green stalked out to the plate. The burning fire that had gripped Chip's heart came to life again, but despite the blinding animosity gripping him, he noticed that Green had moved still farther back in the batter's box. Soapy called for a fastball, but Chip shook him off. He wanted a curveball. The redhead came right back with the sign, and Chip nodded.

He used all of his wrist power to snap a sharp, darting curve to the plate. It came in low and cut around Green's knees for a called strike. He breathed a sigh of relief. He was ahead of the batter. The burly hitter had stepped back out of the box and was knocking the heels of his spikes with his bat.

Soapy wanted another curve, but Chip shook him off until he got the sign for a screwball. Davis was edging off second, but he moved back when Chip checked him. Green was ready in the batter's box when Chip burned his screwball toward the outside corner. The ball took off just before it reached the plate and sailed in toward Green and across the plate. Green whipped his bat down and through, but he didn't connect. Strike two!

Soapy knew exactly what to call next. He gave the sign and Chip nodded grimly. Green would expect him to waste a pitch, to use a teaser out of hitting range. He stepped on the rubber, peered over his shoulder at Davis, and then faked a high hard one. At the last moment his knuckles dipped under the ball, and it barely turned over as it wobbled through the air. It was just the ticket!

Green had been poised and ready for the fastball. The change-up threw him off, but just for a second. He recovered his balance and got set for the kill. The knuckleball dropped down toward the plate, and Green tried to murder it, but his spikes let him down. They slipped from under him, and he lost his balance, missing the ball and falling to the ground.

A yell burst from both dugouts, but it wasn't because of Green's strikeout. It was because of the sudden play at second base that followed the batting incident. Without hesitating a second, Soapy had thrown a clothesline peg to second base and caught Davis flat-footed. The fleet sophomore was trapped in a hopeless rundown situation between Crowell and Morris. The two veterans gradually closed in on him. After a fake toss, Speed easily ran Davis down for the third out.

Chip forgot all about Green and the successful strikeout. He sped after Soapy and slapped him on the back. The redhead's throw had been a big-league play. It had been a risky throw. Everyone knew runners on second often try to draw the throw so they can make a dash for third. Soapy had figured everyone, including Davis, would be engrossed in the duel between Chip and Ben and had flashed the throw sign to Crowell. Fortunately, he had been right. The play had called for a daring decision, and Soapy had been successful.

Team A came running in with cheers for Soapy, but the players were aware that this was their last chance to pull the game out of the fire. Pepping it up, they concentrated their bench jockeying on Dean.

Biggie Cohen led off and lined a clean single up the middle. Red Schwartz walked on six pitches. Murphy Gillen singled to left field. The team A dugout was jumping with the sight of loaded bases. Durley hit Dean's first pitch right on the nose and straight into Foster's glove on the fly. Gillen, thinking the ball had cleared the infield, started for second and was caught diving back to first base by the shortstop's double-up throw.

Two away! There were still men on second and third.

Soapy came up for his second time at bat and waited Dean out. Then, poised in the batter's box with the count at three and one, he checked his swing. Dean's fastball was low and outside for a called ball four.

The bases were loaded with two down!

Chip had been swinging the warm-up bat in the on-deck circle. He tossed it away and picked up his regular bat. Chip knew this was his chance to make up for losing his head during the last inning, and it was the last chance to win the game. Cohen, Schwartz, and Smith took short leads at third, second, and first. All were ready to run as soon as the bat met the ball.

It was now or never. Chip made up his mind to go for it on the first pitch if Dean got the ball over the plate. He wasn't going to make the same mistake he had made the last time either. Chip wasn't trying to knock the ball out of the park.

"No hitter, Diz," Green yelled.

Dean took his stretch. The fastball he fired was a trifle outside and letter-high. Batting righty, Chip pulled his bat through in a full, smooth swing and met the ball solidly. It took off on a low, yet rising, trajectory for right field. Fielder Ricky Gates turned and headed for the fence.

Chip had sprinted for first base, but when he saw the ball shoot over Ricky's head and clear the fence, he slowed down his pace. A quick look showed Red rounding third and heading for home with Soapy almost on his heels. Chip felt a warm glow of satisfaction. He hadn't tried to powder the ball at all. Keeping control of his emotions and timing his swing had paid off! He had learned a valuable lesson.

Green had pivoted with the crack of the bat and now watched the ball's flight. When it sailed over the fence, he slammed his glove down on the ground with all his might. Then, just as Chip tagged the bag and made the turn for second base, Green stepped directly in front of him.

Chip swerved to the outside to avoid Green, but when he saw Ben's sneering face, he gave in to the urge to lash back. "Does that qualify me as a home-run hitter, Ben?" he asked softly.

Green took a step toward him. For a moment Chip thought the disgruntled player was going to tangle with him then and there. But with an obvious effort, the angry first baseman regained his composure. The cocky smile flashed across his tight lips. Chip was caught by surprise, thinking Green wasn't angry until he saw the malicious glare in the big player's light blue eyes. He continued on around second base, tagged third, and trotted to home plate where Biggie, Red, and Soapy were waiting with outstretched hands and congratulations.

Chip shook hands with each of them as his teammates poured out of the dugout. Chip slipped on his warm-up jacket as the entire team hurried toward the locker room.

"That's wrapping it up," Soapy chortled gleefully. "Good thing too," he continued. "We're due at Grayson's in twenty minutes."

"I bet the fountain crowd is lined up three deep," Finley added.

Chip had never felt better in his life. The home-run blow had more than made up for his mental lapse in the bottom of the fourth. He had definitely evened things up with Ben Green too! With Soapy's help, he had exploited the big player's batting weakness and struck him out twice in a row in front of a big-league scout.

The locker room was soon filled with laughter and good-natured ribbing between the teams.

"*Now* I know how to win the games," Speed said lightly to Chip. "Just hit the ball over the fence."

"Wonder boy did it again!"

Ben Green's boisterous voice rang out above the sound and turmoil. "The all-American won his own game!" he jeered as the room quieted. "Chip Hilton always wins the games that way. Don't you guys read the papers? He's State's one-man team!"

Biggie Cohen's head shot up as he looked grimly in Ben Green's direction. After a short, tense moment, he turned away and walked quietly to his locker. There was a brief lull in the conversation, and then the chatter resumed.

Chip said nothing, but his elation had collapsed like a punctured balloon as the reality of the situation dawned on him. He had let himself be drawn into a personal feud with one of his teammates and forgotten the team's well-being and his responsibilities as its captain. When an athlete is elected captain, he is supposed to place the welfare of the team above his own personal glory and gratification.

This is especially a situation to pray about, he told himself. Today he had deliberately set out to show up Ben Green, and in doing so he had placed himself on the same level. He had let the other player's bench jockeying get under his skin and had permitted his personal feelings to take precedent over team spirit—right out in the open for all of his teammates to see.

CHAPTER 5

The Name of the Game

GRAYSON'S, the popular State University collegiate meeting place, was jammed as usual. Soapy groaned as he glanced at the crowd of students lined up in front of the fountain and filling the tables and booths. "Come on, Fireball," he said, heading for the stockroom, "Whitty and the guys are going to kill us!"

With Fireball on his heels, Soapy threaded his way swiftly through the customers in line and at the counters.

Chip waved hello to Mitzi Savrill and paused to talk to several friends at the fountain. Mitzi, a State University student, had worked at Grayson's since her high school days. She was chief assistant to the owner, George Grayson.

By the time Chip reached his work area, the stockroom, Soapy and Fireball had changed into their Grayson's uniforms—white slacks and red and blue polo shirts.

Skip Miller and Lonnie Freeman, part-time high school employees, worked with Chip to inventory and supply both the food court area and the pharmacy side of the business. Chip's two assistants were filling department orders but dropped everything when Chip entered. "What happened?" Skip asked quickly.

"Not much," Soapy answered just as quickly. "We just killed 'em, that's all."

"You mean Chip killed 'em," Fireball corrected.

"I was coming to that," Soapy said. "Anyway, Dugan got into a spot of trouble, and, well, the coach asked me to take over."

"You?" Fireball yelped. "Take over?"

"Well, me and Chip. Anyway, just as soon as we got in the game, Chip struck Ben Green out twice in a row and then cracked a clutch homer to win the game."

Skip's eyes lit up with surprise and pleasure. "Yes!" he said happily. "Am I glad to hear that! Wait till I see Joe."

"Joe who?"

"Joe Green," Skip said, "one of Moose Green's brothers. He plays right field on my team."

Soapy was puzzled. "Moose? Who's Moose?"

"That's what they call Ben Green around town."

"What kind of a person is Joe?" Fireball asked.

"If you know Ben, you know them all," Skip said, grinning. "They all look alike and act alike. They all go for bubble gum too. We call them Ben Bubbles, Joe Bubbles, and Marty Bubbles."

"How about Marty?"

"Another Ben, another bully. At least he tries to act like Ben."

"Did Joe Green ever try to push you around?" Fireball asked curiously.

"He tried," Skip said pointedly, "but I was waiting for him. He hasn't bothered me since."

"Was Ben much of an athlete in high school?" Soapy asked.

Skip nodded. "He was pretty good in baseball and he played football, but I notice he didn't go out for football at State. Anyway, baseball is his best game. He's played with the town team for three or four summers. I never had much to do with Ben, but I—and most everybody else—knows his reputation."

"C'mon Fireball, you're making us late *again*," Soapy urged as he started to walk to the door leading out to the busy food court area.

"Me? I'll be behind the fountain talking to all the girls before you even finish tying your shoes!" Fireball then laughed and nonchalantly bent over to tug at the surprised redhead's shoelaces before running toward the door.

"Very clever, Finley. I used to do that in middle school," Soapy yelled out as Fireball disappeared through the door.

Chip, glad that the evening's entertainment was winding down, sat down in front of his computer and began to work with the perpetual inventory spreadsheets, delivery entries, and packing lists. Skip and Lonnie were putting the day's deliveries on the shelves. Engrossed in his work, Chip didn't even hear George Grayson walk into the room.

Like all Grayson's employees, Chip thought a lot of his boss. George Grayson was a dedicated State University alum and a loyal supporter of the school's many programs. He had worked his way through college, remained in University, and then become one of the college town's most respected community leaders. A large number of his employees were college students who either needed to earn or wanted to earn money for part of their school expenses.

Chip was in charge of the stockroom and also many other behind-the-scenes details that made Grayson's operate efficiently. Chip figured he had the best job of all because he could schedule his work hours around other academic and athletic commitments.

"How was practice?" Grayson asked, looking from Chip to Skip and back again.

"Fine," Chip and Skip chorused, almost as one voice. They looked at each other and grinned. Skip was the star pitcher of the local high school. He had gotten in from practice only a few minutes ahead of Chip.

"Sometimes I can hardly tell you two apart," Grayson said in amazement. "Same blond hair, same gray eyes, and nearly the same build and height."

"Chip's better looking," Lonnie ventured teasingly.

"My mom doesn't think so," said Skip with a laugh. "But I am getting taller and heavier. I'm almost six-three and I'm at 185 pounds, same as Chip."

"Actually, 190 pounds. It's still early in the season," Chip corrected.

"Turn around, you two," Mr. Grayson said. "Stand back to back."

Chip and Skip backed up against each other, and George Grayson eyed the top of their heads. "He's still got you by a hair, Skip," he said kindly.

"Pretty soon I'll have to look up to him," Chip said, smiling.

"That'll be the day," Skip said sincerely, adding more meaning to the discussion.

"I wouldn't worry about that, Skip," Grayson said warmly. "You two resemble each other more than just physically. Well," he added, glancing at the neatly arranged shelves, "I guess I'll go home for supper; you men certainly have everything under control here. Oh, yes, Chip. I nearly forgot. How did the team look in the intrasquad game?"

"Pretty good, Mr. Grayson."

"Better than good," Skip interjected quickly. "At least Chip was! His team won. He hit a game-winning homer with two down in the last inning."

"He has a habit of doing that," Grayson said proudly. "Well, see you two later."

Chip sent Lonnie and Skip out to the fountain for their break and then did some studying. Later, after Skip and Lonnie had gone home, he hit the books again. At 10:30, Soapy and Fireball came back from the fountain, tired and anxious to get home to Jefferson Hall, their dormitory. It took the three of them only half an hour to reach the dormitory and be in bed.

Chip heard Soapy get up the next morning, but he kept quiet. The redhead's morning program never varied. Soapy would beat the alarm by a split second, slip quietly out of bed, pull on his sweats, and jog to the convenience store around the corner. He enjoyed talking with the morning work crew before heading back to Jeff, swooping up the newspapers from the stack piled on the dorm's front porch, and arriving just as Chip finished dressing.

There was no change in the schedule this Thursday morning. After Soapy showered, they set out for the student union building. They walked down to the first floor, out Jeff's door, across the broad, wide porch, and down the long walk to the street. Cutting across the campus, they reached the student union in less than five minutes.

Chip glanced at the table where the guys always assembled for breakfast and saw Biggie, Speed, Red, Fireball, and Whitty. Soapy joined them, but Chip fell in at the end of the cafeteria line. Talking with fellow students and the cafeteria employees, he moved along the line, selecting milk, fruit, juice, a bowl of oatmeal, a plate of wheat toast, and some scrambled eggs. Carrying the tray of food carefully across the room, he sat down at the table. Then, while he ate, he listened to his pals' conversation.

Between bites of breakfast, Soapy read aloud from the sports page of the *News*. But, as usual, his companions were ignoring him and talking among themselves.

"Listen to this!" the redhead exclaimed. "Listen to what Jim Locke has in his column." He paused and waited until he got their attention again.

"Hey, are you guys listening?" he complained. "Listen to what Locke writes: 'I have never seen a State University baseball team with as much hitting power and all-around fielding class as Coach Henry Rockwell's current Statesmen.

The squad is loaded with long-ball sluggers and defensive stars.'"

Soapy pounded the table and glared at Speed, who had muttered something to Biggie. "Pay attention, knucklehead!" he barked, glaring at his old friend. "Listen, you guys: 'If there is a weakness, it is in the pitching department.

"'Anyone who knows baseball will tell you that pitching is the name of the game and that good pitching will always beat good hitting. Chip Hilton is the best college pitcher in the country, but he can't pitch all the games. There's the rub. If Hank Rockwell can cure Diz Dean's wildness, he will have the best one-two mound punch in the country. Ninety percent of a great pitcher's repertoire is his fastball—*if* he can control it. Diz Dean has the fastball, all right, but he's as likely to throw it over the grandstand as the plate.'"

"That's a big if!" exclaimed Red.

"Yep," Biggie said, rising. "Don't any of you guys have classes? It's getting late."

All of them had classes, and Biggie's directive sent them scurrying in several directions. Chip had three morning classes in a row. He had a quick lunch and then spent an hour in the Metcalf Library. Next he hustled over to the Ward Lanham Science Center for his two-hour chemistry lab. The chimes of the campus clock on the student union tower ended his school day at three. He was glad to get out in the sunshine and head for Alumni Field.

The only person in the locker room was Bobby Traymore, the student manager. He checked Chip's reporting time in the roll book and went back to sorting uniforms. Chip dressed swiftly and ran out on the field just as Coach Rockwell was assembling the players in the third-base bleachers.

Stu Gardner joined Coach Henry Rockwell. The two men waited quietly until the players were seated. Rockwell stepped forward and addressed the group. "Men," he said proudly, "I'm sure some of you have recognized Stu Gardner. Stu is chief scout of the Yankees organization and an old friend of mine. I've asked him to talk to you about organized baseball in general and about big-league recruiting of college players in particular. After that, you might have some questions. His visit with us is purely informative and is approved by the NCAA."

Rockwell turned to the scout. "Stu, welcome to State University baseball," he said. "It's all yours."

The team gave Gardner a round of applause. He was tall, slender, tanned, and apparently in excellent health. His black hair was threaded with gray, and his brown eyes were keen and alert.

"Thanks, Rock," Gardner said. "Men, it's a real pleasure to talk with you today and be with my old friend, Coach Rockwell. Professional clubs rely on college players to a great extent to fill their rosters. Because of this there used to be a lot of abuses in making contact with college players.

"Coach Rockwell thought you might be interested in some of the restrictions governing a scout's relationship with college ballplayers. Professional baseball, or rather its representatives, have often been accused of appropriating college players. College authorities and particularly college coaches have been up in arms over the problem for years. In many instances, there were justifiable complaints.

"To fight the problem, the commissioner of baseball and the club owners have been working on legislation with the NCAA to protect the players, colleges, and organized baseball.

"Probably the most important restriction they have come up with is the clause that prohibits any club official, scout, or employee from directly or indirectly inducing a student to refrain from playing college ball. This includes inducing a player to withdraw from college to play professional ball or to transfer to another college. This is part of the so-called College Rule.

"The penalty for violation of the College Rule is an immediate voiding of the contract, if one was signed. Furthermore, the offending club is prohibited from signing the player concerned for three additional years. Any major-league clubs or their minor-league affiliates are subject to large monetary fines and sanctions. We, and the NCAA, have very strict guidelines regarding the drafting of players at the collegiate and high school levels.

"The commissioner or the president of the national association also can fine individual scouts, sports agents, and other employees." Gardner paused and looked around the group. "Are there any questions about this rule?" he asked.

Soapy rose quickly to his feet. "Yes, Mr. Gardner," he said, "there is. Has this College Rule been in effect very long?"

Gardner nodded. "Yes, several years."

"Well, would the Yankees try to sign a player while he was in college?"

"Absolutely not!"

Chip knew what Soapy was digging for and glanced at Ben Green. Ben's face was fiery red, and he was scowling fiercely. Chip wished Soapy would sit down, but the redhead wasn't about to.

"Well, then, would anyone connected with the Yankees try to get a college player to sign a contract?"

Gardner shook his head vigorously. "Decidedly not. I know every person in the organization. They wouldn't even consider it. That's what the draft is for. Does that clear it up for you?"

"Yes, *sir*," Soapy said pointedly. He looked at Green a moment and then sat down, elbowing Chip in the process.

There was a short, awkward silence, and then Coach Rockwell broke the ice. "You've been watching us for a couple of days, Stu," he said. "Would you mind telling us what you have observed about our fielding and hitting?"

Gardner chuckled and shook his head. "That's kinda putting me on the spot, isn't it, Rock?" He walked back and forth a couple of times and thought it over. "Well," he said, checking his stride, "let me say first that the Yankees are interested in a player here and have been for a long time. It's no secret, as far as I know. We've been watching Chip Hilton ever since he was in high school. And, as far as that's concerned, we've had an eye on another of Coach Rockwell's players."

"No wonder I've been getting so many phone calls," Soapy whispered loudly.

Gardner smiled and continued. "When an organization is interested in a player, its scouts look him over many, many times. They check his physical makeup, speed, hitting, fielding, throwing, and emotional qualities. The check is made by a number of scouts at different times and in different situations. However, they don't try to sign the player or make him an offer until he has graduated from college and declared himself eligible for the draft.

"Regarding fielding, I like to call it defensive play. For a college club, you men seem to be exceptionally strong in the field. You have good arms, and so far I haven't noticed anyone failing to make the right play in a given situation. That shows you're thinking baseball and figuring out the possibilities.

"Now for the hitting: you have plenty of power. But—I hesitate to say this—some of you are swinging too hard. Nothing, but nothing, destroys timing more than forcing a swing.

"Next, let's take speed. When a player runs out a hit or a bunt, he should never go less than all out to first base. Good speed is a tremendous asset. And the only way to develop speed on the bases is to run just the way you would in a game. I'll be here tomorrow to see you play your opening game, and I hope to see a little more speed on the bases. By the way, A & M has a couple of first-class pitchers."

Gardner paused and pulled a stopwatch out of his pocket. "It might interest you to know," he continued, "that I have clocked the speed of most of you a number of times between home plate and first base. So far, the best time has been from the right side of the plate—naturally—three and three-tenths seconds."

"And I have a bad ankle," Soapy murmured audibly.

"From the way some of you run," Gardner said pointedly, "there must be an epidemic of sprained ankles. Now, if you want something to shoot at, a goal within your reach as collegiate players, I've got one. The great Mickey Mantle's best time down to first was three and two-tenths seconds. That was when his knees were in good shape."

"Which one of us made the best time?" someone asked.

Gardner looked questioningly at Rockwell. "Do you mind, Rock?"

"Go ahead," Rockwell encouraged.

"Speed Morris had the best time from the third-base side of the plate," Gardner said. "He made it in three and a half seconds. Hilton got down to first from the righty side of the plate in just over three and a half seconds. That's a great time this early in the season."

"*Everything* Hilton does is great!" Ben Green muttered in a low voice, but loud enough for the team to hear.

Chip shook his head slowly. *I can't win with this guy,* he thought sadly.

CHAPTER 6

Signs of "Inside" Baseball

CHIP HILTON tried to listen to gray-bearded, stocky Professor Bruckman. He tried again to focus his thoughts on the science lecture, but it was impossible. Dr. Bruckman was one of his favorite professors, but today all Chip could think about was the game, and the tight feeling that gripped his chest wouldn't go away. He held his breath, breathed deeply five or six times, and tried to think about something else. It was no use. His thoughts kept rushing back to A & M. In desperation he made a sketch of Dr. Bruckman standing in front of the whiteboard, twirling his gold-rimmed eyeglasses, but it didn't help.

After what seemed like interminable hours, the fifty-minute lecture ended. He picked up his books, packed his backpack, and forced himself to move slowly out of the room. He wanted to run, to get relief through action, but he held back and walked at a moderate pace through the hall and down the steps of the science building. Classmates and students he did not know spoke to him as he crossed the campus. He returned each greeting with a forced smile or a nod.

"Good luck this afternoon, Chip."

"We'll be out there rooting, Hilton."

"Start us out on the right foot!"

In the distance, the flags were rippling gently above the grandstand at Alumni Field. There wasn't a cloud in the sky. Chip quickened his pace and then realized he was stretching his legs as far and as fast as they would go. *Slow down,* he told himself, *you're as nervous as a cat.*

He slowed his pace but couldn't slow his thoughts. He hadn't been on the mound in a real game for a year. *What if I'm not on and don't have what it takes?*

The student attendant at the players' entrance opened the wire gate and slapped him on the back. "The Aggies are already on the field," he said. "You going to take 'em?"

"We're going to try."

The gatekeeper grinned. "Campus gossip says, 'Hilton pitches, State wins.'"

Chip smiled and continued on to the locker room. The chatter and lighthearted ribbing and jokes flying among the players spelled out their confidence, but Chip knew it was mostly for show. The team felt the same way he did. He dressed swiftly, stretching the muscles of his legs and arms and back as he bent over to lace up his spikes. Settling back on the bench, he tried to recall as much as possible about the A & M players.

A little later, Coach Rockwell and Coach Malone appeared, and the trainer, Murph Kelly, shouted for attention. The coaches moved over in front of the white board and the players gathered around them, some sitting on the benches, others leaning against lockers and tables. Soapy crowded in between Chip and Biggie.

"All right. Men," Rockwell said crisply, "by mutual agreement this is only a seven-inning game, but we've still got to hurry. A & M will have had their batting and fielding practice when we get out on the field. Coach Price and I have reversed the usual procedure to save time. We'll take our batting and infield practice as soon as we go out."

The coach pulled a piece of paper from his pocket and read off the names of the starting lineup. "Crowell leads off; Morris hits second; Finley, third; Cohen, fourth; Schwartz, fifth; Gillen, sixth; Durley, seventh; Engle, eighth; and Sparks, ninth."

Soapy released his breath with a quick gasp, and there was a restless shifting of feet by several players. Rockwell held up a hand. "I intended to start Chip today, but Coach Price is going to use his number-two pitcher, Mickey Grove. That means he will use Ed Crowe tomorrow. I prefer to meet strength with strength. Ed Crowe is one of the best hurlers we will face all year.

"Today's A & M pitcher, Grove, is a southpaw. He has a fastball, a good change-up, and a curveball he throws at several speeds to keep the hitters off balance." Rockwell paused, glanced thoughtfully around the circle of faces, and then continued pointedly. "We can get to him *if* you remember what Stu Gardner said about swinging too hard.

"Nickels! Warm up Sparks and Dugan. Dean, pitch to the hitters. Smith, take the plate, on the double now! Let's go out there with a lot of hustle."

Chip had felt the disappointment well up in Soapy. He controlled his feelings, but he felt the same way. He had been counting on pitching the opening game. As the number-one pitcher, he had been expected to start. For a brief moment he felt hurt and rebellious, but only for a moment. *There I go again,* he gritted to himself. *There I go thinking about myself. The Rock knows what he's doing.*

He bowed his head slightly and prayed, saying he was sorry for focusing on himself and that he needed help in leading the team. *Help me to do this, Lord,* he prayed.

Chip slapped Soapy on the back and sprang to his feet. "All right, guys!" he said. "We can't win 'em all if we don't win the first one. Let's do it!"

Leading the way out to the field, he dropped his warm-up jacket on the grass near the dugout and trotted to left field. The home-run kids were lined up behind the fence and they called to him.

"Hey! Number 19! Aren't you Chip Hilton?"

"What are you doing out here? Aren't you gonna pitch today?"

He waved to them and tossed a ball around with Burke, Donovan, and Gates while he waited for the starting lineup hitters to take their hits. The reserve infielders were firing a ball around the horn while they waited, and Soapy was warming Dean up in front of the dugout.

Crowell led off in the batting order. Each starter followed his example: hitting two, laying one down, and running it out. The bell clanged just as they finished their second hitting cycle. Chip raced the outfield chasers back to the dugout, picked up his warm-up jacket, and sat down in the dugout. The starters ran out to their positions, and Sparks began to throw to Engle in front of the dugout.

With Soapy covering the plate, Coach Rockwell hit sharp grounders to Biggie, Crowell, Speed, and Durley. The infield stars fielded the grounders swiftly and surely and threw strikes when they pegged the ball around the horn.

Coach Bill Malone was fungoing high flies to Schwartz, Finley, and Gillen, and the trio made the tough catches look easy. Just then, while Chip watched, Malone lifted a low-rising drive far to Fireball's left. It was a mighty clout, and the ball looked as though it would drop far over the center fielder's head. The fleet outfielder pulled it in with a last-second stab. Fireball could move!

"Bring it in!" Rockwell called, rapping a sharp grounder down the first-base line.

Biggie dashed in, scooped up the ball, and pegged it to Soapy, low and on the third-base side of the plate. He followed his throw and continued on in to the dugout. Rockwell then hit to Crowell, Morris, and Durley in turn.

Each of the infielders handled the ball faultlessly and followed each stop with hard, targeted throws to the plate. The coach then drove several long, low drives to Gillen, Fireball, and Schwartz in the outfield. They fired the ball back to the plate with accurate one-bounce hops. Soapy didn't even have to move. It was a classy performance.

The groundskeepers hustled out on the field with their equipment to smooth out the diamond. The fans gave them a boisterous reception as Chip glanced at the clock on the scoreboard. It was almost time. At three o'clock the plate umpire walked onto the field and announced the State battery. Then it was time. "Play ball!" he announced.

The starting Statesmen sped onto the field while Soapy played catch with Sparks until Engle was ready. The A & M leadoff hitter stepped up to the plate. Fireball started the Statesmen's chatter with his usual call, "Hey, hey, hey there!"

Chip leaned back in the dugout and got ready to check out the A & M hitters.

Sparks's first pitch was a high fastball. The batter, hitting righty, went for it. He got a piece of the ball and fouled it back toward the screen. Engle pivoted, tossed away his mask, and made the catch. One away!

Chip breathed a sigh of relief. Sparks was off to a good start. The number two hitter looked at an outside curveball and tried to lay the next pitch down, but the throw was high, and he fouled it off. On the one-and-one pitch, he met the ball solidly, sending it on a line between Finley and Gillen. The ball rolled all the way to the fence, but Finley's throw held the runner at third.

That brought up the power hitters. The third batter met the first pitch right on the nose, lifting a high fly to Schwartz in left field. Red pulled in the ball, and the third-base runner, after tagging up, beat the throw to home plate by several steps to score the first run of the game.

The Aggies batter in the cleanup slot was tall and powerfully built. He and Sparks played cat and mouse until the count was three and one. Flash didn't want to give up the walk and fired his fastball across the middle. The big player's bat met the ball solidly. The crack of the bat carried authority, and the ball took off low but rose steadily. It cleared the right-field fence easily. The home-run kids had another ball!

Chip groaned to himself when the big 2 rolled into place on the scoreboard.

The fifth batter flied out, and the Statesmen came running in for their turn at bat. The Aggies were full of pep as they trotted out on the field and tossed the ball around. Grove looked loose, poised, and sure, and the lefty's confidence was obvious in every move he made.

Crowell walked. Morris bunted, and the catcher threw him out at first. Crowell advanced to second. Fireball dug in and looked at two balls and a strike. Then he smashed a hanging curveball toward left field. It looked like the ball was in there for a sure hit. Crowell took off for third base, but the Aggies shortstop leaped high in the air and speared the ball! Twisting in the air, he fired the ball to second base in time to catch Crowell with the double-up throw. Three away!

A & M scored two more runs in its half of the second frame, and the score was 4-0 when the Statesmen came in for their turn at bat. Biggie, batting righty against Grove's southpaw pitching, looked at three breaking pitches in a row. He watched the first one go by for a called strike and took a vicious cut at the second. The third curve was low, and the umpire called it a ball. With the count one and two, Grove fired his slider. It shot in under Biggie's wrists, and he was out on a called strike.

Schwartz hit a hard-liner to the visitors' left fielder for the second out. Gillen's smash to right field was just short of the fence, and the Aggies right fielder pulled it in for the third out.

The visitors hit Sparks hard in the next three innings, but his defensive support was flawless, and the Aggies failed to score. Grove had the Statesmen eating out of his hand in the bottom of the third and fourth innings. But in the fifth, Morris walked and Finley doubled to left field.

With Morris on third and Fireball poised on second, Coach Rockwell called time and sent Green up to bat for Cohen. Then Rockwell told Burke to get ready to hit for Schwartz. Green had been sitting at the far end of the dugout. When Rockwell called him, he put on a "surprised" act.

Walking out to the bat rack, Green took his time select-ing a bat. Then, picking up the weighted bat, he clasped the two bats with his right hand and swung them around his head several times. Transferring them to his left hand, he repeated the process. Tossing the weighted bat away, he stalked up to the plate.

The plate umpire faced the grandstand and bellowed, "Green, batting for Cohen."

Pulling on his mask, the umpire waited for Green to step into the box, but the burly first baseman wasn't ready. Chewing methodically on the big wad of gum in his mouth, he started his regular batting ritual and, despite the bench jockeying from the Aggies dugout, took his time. After fin-ishing the familiar routine, he looked covertly toward the third-base coaching box.

Rockwell always gave the signs from the dugout. Each time the Statesmen came in to bat, the player who had bat-ted last in the previous inning would sit on the coach's right. Rock would give the plays to this player. Then, just as the batter advanced to the plate, Coach Rockwell would say, "Now," and the designated player would flash the sign to the third-base coach. Simultaneously, Rockwell would look toward third base and fake all sorts of signs. Chip had long ago recognized the value of Rock's unique method of teach-ing signs and "inside" baseball to his players.

Coach Malone was moving about in the coaching box, eager to have the game resume. He took off his cap, dusted it against his thigh, put it back on his head, and clapped his hands. "C'mon, big boy!" he cried. "Step up there and get ahold of one."

The Rock had given the play to Crowell, and when Green moved toward the batter's box, he told Crowell to give the hit-away sign to Malone. The coach flashed the sign to Green, and Chip saw Green dig in. Green was set to knock the ball out of sight. It struck Chip that Grove might have been annoyed by all of Green's batting preliminaries, and he wondered whether the southpaw would brush Ben back from the plate.

He wasn't kept in doubt very long. Grove reared back and blazed a high fastball straight toward the inside corner. The pitch was high and close, but Green exaggerated the nearness. He tossed the bat back over his head and fell away from the plate, obviously upset. Then his spikes caught in the clay and he fell flat on his back. The spill drew a roar of laughter from the grandstand and both dugouts.

Green scrambled to his feet and grabbed the bat in one hand and his helmet in the other, his face as red as fire. He took a step toward the mound and lifted the bat as if to throw it at Grove. Then, choking with anger, he pivoted around and glared at the umpire. After a moment of hesitation, he walked back until his face was no more than a foot from the umpire's mask. "Beanball, ump!" he shouted. "He tried to bean me!"

The umpire took off his mask, shook his head, and said something quietly to Green. Then, turning away, he cried "Play ball!" and took his place behind the catcher. Green looked toward the dugout and then back at the umpire. After stealing a quick glance at Coach Malone, he stepped back in the box and banged his bat on the plate.

CHAPTER 7

Bull Pen Scapegoat

"DUCKS ON the pond, Ben," Burke cried from the on-deck circle.

The A & M pitcher eyed Morris edging off third, took his stretch, hesitated in the hold position, and then delivered. The pitch was inside again, just under Green's elbows. Ball two!

"Make him pitch to you, Big Ben," Coach Malone yelled.

Grove started the next pitch way outside, but it cut in and hooked around Green's shoulders for a called strike. Then, for the first time, the Aggies pitcher came in with one around Green's knees. Chip leaned forward to watch and caught himself nodding when Green fouled it off.

The two-and-two pitch was an inside, waist-high curve, and Green teed off. The solid crack of the bat spelled distance, and Chip knew that this one was tagged, labeled to go all the way. Speed and Fireball knew it, too, and were on their way home long before the ball cleared the left-field fence.

The ball carried squarely over the four-hundred-foot mark. The delighted yelps of the home-run kids positioned beyond the fence could be heard in the dugout.

The fans cheered Green all the way around the bases. Speed and Fireball waited at home plate to greet him with the traditional home-run handshake and high-five, but Green, who was busily waving to the fans, passed them up without a thought and swaggered to the dugout.

Belter Burke had been in the on-deck circle. He also tried to grasp Green's hand, but the first baseman was too absorbed in the grandstand demonstration and brushed right past him. When the cheering died down, Burke, batting righty, moved to the plate and got set. The home-run kids were still parked behind the left-field fence.

Grove sent a shoulder-high fastball through; it was a little on the first-base side of the plate, and Belter whaled away at it. He was a bit late, but the ball took off like a rocket for the right-field fence. The kids began the long chase to right field as Burke trotted around the bases. The fans gave the powerful slugger a great ovation when he crossed the plate with the tying run. It was a new ball game!

Gillen tried to keep the home-run barrage going, but he was swinging from his heels, and Grove set him down one-two-three on two curves and a slider. Durley grounded out. Engle pulled a high fly to the Aggies left fielder to retire the side. The score: A & M 4, State 4.

Back in the ball game now, the Statesmen charged out on the field full of fire. Sparks got off to a bad start with his first pitch and hit the leadoff batter. He walked the second. The third batter bunted and was safe when Sparks fumbled the ball. With the bases loaded and no one down, Rockwell called time and walked to the mound. He talked with Engle and Sparks for a few minutes and then waved an arm toward the bull pen. Dugan walked in slowly. Sparks shook his head with resignation and made the long, lonely trek to the dugout. The fans gave him a big hand, but his chin was riding his knees when he dropped down beside Chip on the bench.

"Don't worry about it, Flash," Chip said softly, using the player's nickname. "We'll get 'em!"

"I screwed up my big chance," Sparks said bitterly.

"There will be other chances," Chip said gently, "lots of them before the season is over."

Dugan tried desperately to put out the fire, but the wrinkle on his curveball was missing. His slider hung in the air just right for smacking. The first hitter picked one off like an apple on a tree, driving the ball directly over Speed's head. The ball hit the grass and rolled all the way to the fence before Fireball could retrieve it. His throw reached the infield in time to hold the hitter on third, but the triple had cleared the bases and three runners had scored.

The next Aggie flied out to Gillen, but the third-base runner beat the throw to the plate for another run. Dugan was upset and couldn't find the plate. He walked the next batter on four straight pitches. With one away and a runner on first, the Aggies tried the hit and run. Crowell started toward the bag as if to take the throw. The batter punched the ball toward the opening between first and second.

Ozzie Crowell and Speed Morris had their fake cover play nailed down to perfection. When Crowell cut back to field the ball, Speed covered the bag. Ozzie fielded the ball. His throw to Speed forced the runner at second base, and Speed's throw to Green completed the double play and retired the side. The score: 8-4.

The Statesmen were desperate when they hustled in for their at bats in the bottom of the sixth. They needed some runs, and fast! Rockwell sent Nickels in to hit for Dugan and told Dean to warm up with Soapy. The tall lefty walked out to the bull pen beyond third base and went to work.

Nickels, batting righty, hit a double to left field on the first pitch. Crowell flied out to center field. The Aggies outfielder held Nickels on second. Morris singled then and Nickels went to third. With one down and runners on first and third, Rockwell called time and sent Ricky Gates out of the dugout to hit for Finley.

Gates, a righty hitter, looked at a ball and a called strike and then swung at one of Grove's curves with all his strength. He got hold of the ball, and it blazed over the Aggies second baseman's head. It landed in right center on the grass and kept going. Nickels scored easily. Speed turned second, and it looked like he would go all the way, but the Aggies center fielder pegged the ball to home plate. Coach Malone held Speed at third. Gates took advantage of the throw to move on to second.

The fans gave Green a standing ovation as he strode to the plate, and Ben ate it up. He transferred the big wad of bubble gum from one cheek to the other and went through all his batting rituals slowly. Before he could enter the batter's box, the A & M coach called for time. Walking out to the mound, he huddled with the Aggies battery.

"They're going to put him on," Chip muttered to himself, "and that'll fill the bases. They'll set up a play at any base."

He was right. Grove threw four consecutive pitches outside the reach of Green's bat, and the catcher stepped out from behind the plate each time to make the catches. Green put on a big show of disappointment. He savagely threw his bat down on the ground, pulled off his batting helmet, and carried it in his hands as he trotted slowly down to first base, glowering at Grove all the while. The bases were loaded now, and Rockwell called time as the tying run stood on first base.

Burke, standing in the on-deck circle, listened closely as Rockwell talked to him briefly. Turning back to the dugout, Coach Rockwell called for Donovan to get ready to hit for Gillen. The Rock was right on that move, Chip thought easily. Gillen couldn't buy a hit.

Grove was worried, and Speed tried to keep him that way. The lefty hurler was facing toward first base, so Speed could afford to take a bigger lead. He began kicking up the dust and dancing off the base, trying to draw a throw. Grove ignored him and appeared to be concentrating on Burke. Biggie, coaching at first, and Malone, standing in the third-base box, were very alert, talking to the runners and watching Grove closely. The lefty pitched carefully to Burke. The count went to two and one.

Grove got the sign for the next pitch, toed the rubber, and took his stretch. Lowering his arms, he looked over his right shoulder to check Speed.

Then it happened!

Chip saw it coming and cried out at the top of his lungs. "Green!" he yelled frantically, "Get back!"

It was too late. In a blur of movement, Grove suddenly turned to first base and pegged the ball to the bag. The burly runner made a desperate attempt to get back to the bag, but the pickoff throw was perfect, low and on the second base side. Ben was out by a good three feet. He turned immediately and began yelling at Biggie, but the line coach wasn't having any of that! Biggie turned his back and walked away from his angry rival.

Green came back to the dugout talking to himself. There were no cheers from the fans now. Instead, many of them razzed him with every step he made.

"You sleepy, bubbles?"

"Wake up, Moose!"

"If you wanna watch the game, sit in the bleachers!"

The Aggies coach was out of the dugout again and took a long look at Grove. He didn't call time, and Chip sighed in relief. They were going to pitch to Belter.

The next pitch was low and outside, bringing the count to three and one. Now Chip understood the strategy. They weren't going to give Belter anything good, and they were trying to coax him to go for a bad pitch. Chip grinned to himself. The Aggies didn't know Burke. They would have to bring 'em in for Belter.

Grove came in with an outside pitch once more, and the umpire waved Burke to first base. Belter tossed his bat away and trotted down to the bag. The bases were loaded once more. Donovan, carrying the potential winning run, came up for the first time.

"Two away, guys," the Aggies shortstop yelled. "Play at any base." Donovan got set, and Grove tried a curveball. The careful batter looked it over and passed it up. Ball one. Grove came back with another breaker for a called strike. Donovan hardly moved in the box but stood with his bat in the ready position, concentrating on the pitcher. This time Grove blazed his fastball in, and Donovan took a hard swing. He connected, sending a line drive over the second baseman's head and to the left of the center fielder.

Speed and Gates were off and running. Speed scored easily, but Gates had to hit the dirt to beat the relay throw. Donovan made it to second on the play at the plate.

The fans were standing and yelling for another hit when Andre Durley stepped into the box. Grove worked carefully on the stocky third baseman and the count reach two and two. Then it happened again!

Grove checked Donovan, took his stretch, lowered the ball to the hold position, and then pivoted suddenly and threw to the second baseman. Donovan was caught sound asleep, and the Aggies infielder ran him down for the third out. The score at the end of six innings: A & M 8, State 7.

Rodney "Diz" Dean walked out to the rubber to take his warm-up throws. Bobby Traymore penciled in the change on a piece of paper and took it out to the plate umpire. The umpire waited until Dean finished his throws and then announced the change.

Soapy started in from the bull pen, but Rockwell waved him back and beckoned to Chip. "Throw a few," he said briefly.

Chip picked up his glove and started for the bull pen. Rock was going all out and that meant he thought the game could be won. Chip felt the same way.

Soapy was waiting with his catcher's mitt. "Better hurry," he said, shaking his head ruefully. "If I know anything about baseball, I know what's coming for sure."

"What?" Chip asked, keeping an eye on the game.

"Diz is gonna blow as high as a kite."

"Why do you say that?"

"It's the first game and he's nervous. Besides, he isn't right. C'mon, start throwing!"

Chip started his throws, watching the developments as he warmed up. Green, Crowell, and Morris had circled Dean and were talking to him. Now they fanned out to their positions, and the lefty faced his first A & M hitter.

Dean got off to a good start. He smoked in two of his fastballs, which were good for called strikes, but then he made three bad throws in a row. The batter swung at the next pitch, a cripple, and sent a slow roller down the first-base line. It should have been an easy out. Dean fielded the ball well but lost his balance when he pivoted to make his lefty throw. He forced the toss, and the ball flew over Green's head and out to right field. Gates had backed up the play, and his throw to Crowell held the runner at first.

"Better hurry!" Soapy said grimly.

Soapy was right. Dean walked the next hitter, putting men on first and second with no one down. Chip began to throw a little faster, fearful Rock might have to wave him in before he was ready.

The next batter was up at the plate with obvious instructions to look them over. He worked Dean to three and one. Dean threw one of his southpaw curveballs then, and the Aggies couldn't get out of the way in time. The ball plunked solidly into his back, and the umpire waved him down to first base. Rockwell called time and walked out to the mound to huddle with Engle and Dean.

"Here you come," Soapy warned.

Just then, Rockwell turned and waved him in. Chip pulled on his warm-up jacket and started for the infield. Soapy sat down on the bench in the bull pen and shook his fist in the air for good luck, but Rockwell was still waving and Chip stopped.

"He wants Soapy too," Donovan called.

Soapy shot out like a sprinter from the starting blocks. "Let's go!" he barked as he passed by Chip. "Let's go win this ball game!"

Chip pulled off his warm-up jacket when he reached the dugout and waited for Rockwell's instructions. Rodney Dean passed by at that instant. Chip tried to cheer him up. "Don't worry about it, Diz," he said sympathetically.

"I *won't!*" Dean said bitterly. "Let's see how you like being a bull pen scapegoat."

CHAPTER 8

A Sudden Inspiration

DIZ DEAN'S remark was completely out of character for the lefty pitcher. He was normally lighthearted and friendly, and Chip was truly caught by surprise. Trapped between thoughts of the game and Diz's attitude, he was thrown completely off balance. He tried to think of something to say but couldn't find the words.

Rockwell solved the problem. He grasped Chip by the arm. "Hold 'em down, Chip," he said gently. "We'll get the runs for you."

On his way to the pitcher's mound, Chip's thoughts flew back to the preceding summer. This would be the first time he had been on the mound in a real game since the previous August, when he had pitched against Keio University in Tokyo. The trip to South Korea and Japan had followed State's victorious march to the NCAA championship. He smiled ruefully as he recalled how the Statesmen had lost out in the Japanese college tournament. *Well, that was last year,* he mused.

Soapy, clad in his catching gear, signaled to Chip to take his warm-up throws. Chip did so and then walked partway down the alley to join the redhead for the unnecessary formality of checking their signs. He and Soapy knew the signs by heart. Together they had played sandlot baseball and even T-ball as elementary school kids. Now they often knew what the other was thinking before even speaking.

"Bases loaded, no one down," Soapy warned. "There's a good hitter coming up. Watch for a bunt."

The redhead retreated to the plate, and Chip walked back to the mound. Facing the outfield, he noted that the home-run kids had changed their tactics. Now they were strung out thirty or forty feet apart clear around the outside of the steel-wire fence. He sure didn't want to help their collection efforts now!

The umpire made the introduction, and Chip faced the plate. The old familiar chatter began as he checked the runners, and even Ben Green got into the spirit, calling, "Throw the ball in there! We'll do the rest!"

The first batter to face him was a righty hitter, and he was batting in the second spot. Chip decided to keep his pitches high and nodded when Soapy signaled for a fastball around the shoulders. But right at that instant he had a sudden inspiration. Rubbing the ball across the letters of his shirt, he shook Soapy off.

Soapy stood up and placed glove and meat hands on his hips. Waiting quietly for a moment, he thumped his fist into his glove several times and squatted. He gave the sign Chip wanted. Watching the runner on third base closely, Chip took a full windup and came in with his fastball shoulder-high and two feet outside, in perfect position for a catcher's peg.

Durley and Green advanced toward the plate with the pitch, ready to make a play at home. Speed sprinted up behind the third-base runner just as the fastball cracked into Soapy's glove. The redhead played it perfectly, turning his head toward third and cocking his arm. The Aggies coach in the third-base box yelled frantically, and the runner dove back to the bag.

The first-base runner was watching the action at third base. Soapy's sudden throw toward first base caught him flat-footed. Crowell had come up behind him on the dead run, took Soapy's throw, and tagged the bewildered runner before he realized what had happened. The lead runner on third faked a dash for home, but Ozzie came running in with the ball, poised for the throw, and the Aggies retreated to the bag. One away!

Chip shook his head in admiration. It was the sort of inside baseball that had helped them win the championship the previous year. He turned to look toward second base. Fireball had covered the bag on the play. Now the center fielder threw a quick salute toward him and trotted back to his position. Soapy had flashed the sign for the play to Crowell, and Ozzie had relayed it on out to Fireball. It was real teamwork, and his heart thumped with pride.

The batter was back up at the plate now, and Soapy called for a high fast one. The throw was just above the shoulders, and the batter was ahead of him. He figured, just as Soapy had, that the Aggies wanted a run to protect their lead. Soapy called for a fastball again, and Chip fired it in, shoulder-high and a bit on the outside.

Durley and the third-base runner raced in almost side by side as the batter whirled and bunted the ball. The ball had been hit too hard, and Durley took it on the first bounce. Durley threw a strike low and right above the sliding runner to Soapy who was blocking the plate. The dust swirled up as the runner hit the dirt, but Soapy's tag was sure and hard, and the umpire jerked his thumb over his shoulder.

Two away! But there were men on first and third.

The third-spot hitter took his time getting ready and gave Chip time to recall what the Aggies hitter had done so far at the plate. The tall hitter had flied out the first time, beat out a bunt for a hit in the third inning, and tripled in the fifth. He was a versatile batter.

The cleanup hitter was standing in the on-deck circle. He

had hit the first home run of the game. Chip had watched him carefully each time he batted. Comparing the two, he decided the cleanup hitter was the less dangerous. He shook Soapy off until he got the walk sign and carefully threw four straight balls out of the batter's reach. The versatile batter walked, and the Aggies on first moved down to second. The bases were full once more.

The cleanup batter was tall and powerful. He stood well back in the first-base side of the box and used a wide stance. Soapy called for a low curveball, and Chip blazed it in around the batter's knees for a called strike. He wasted an outside fastball and came back with a curveball that was too close. Two and one! Soapy wanted a wide curveball, but Chip shook him off until he got the sign for a knuckler. Faking his fastball, he came in with the knuckler.

The big player had been set for the heat, but he recovered quickly and got set to powder the ball. He hit it solidly, sending a hard shot directly toward Crowell. The ball was too hot to handle, but Ozzie knocked it down. Diving for the ball, he scooped it up and whipped it to second base. Speed timed his move just right and caught the ball as he cut across the bag. The Aggies runner's slide took Speed out on the play, but the ball had beaten the runner to the bag, and the base umpire threw his arm in the air. Carrying the ball in his glove, Speed came running in to the dugout.

Three brilliant plays by his teammates had pulled the Statesmen out of a serious situation. Once again Chip's heart swelled with pride. A hurler had real defensive backing when he pitched for this crew!

Traymore met him with his warm-up jacket and patted him on the back. His teammates came hustling in on the run and added their voices to those of the fans who were rooting for some runs. It was now or never!

In the bottom of the seventh inning, Durley was still up at bat. He had been at the plate when the pickoff play had retired the Statesmen in the bottom of the sixth. Andre now walked out to the plate with the potential tying run, and the fans backed him up with their cheers and applause. The talented third baseman crowded the plate, went into a crouch, and worked Grove for a walk. Now the tying run was on first base, and everyone in the park knew the play. Durley was a streak on the base paths, and it was up to Soapy to advance him to second base.

Chip moved into the on-deck circle and watched Soapy as he swung the warm-up bat. The redhead had a good eye, and any pitcher he faced had to put the ball right in the strike zone if he wanted Soapy to go for it. The Aggies first and third basemen came in with the pitch, but the ball was too high. Soapy let it go by. The second was low, nearly in the dirt, and the count was two and zero. This was it! Grove had to come in there with the next pitch.

Grove shook his receiver off and then brought in his crossfire fastball. It fairly jumped as it reached the plate and went spinning right at Soapy's head. The redhead ducked, but he couldn't get away from the ball, and it plunked into his left shoulder.

Chip knew Soapy must be hurting, but no one else could tell because of the wide grin on the redhead's freckled face. Rubbing his shoulder, he trotted down to first base. Soapy would have stuck his head in front of the ball if it would have helped the team!

Two on, no one down, one run behind. Chip walked slowly toward the plate as the fans gave him a big hand. The Aggies fielders began their chatter.

"Big play at third, guys!"

"Strike him out, Mickey!"

"Easy pickings, lefty."

Yes, Chip mused, pitchers usually *were* easy pickings. Well, they would just see about that.

Malone flashed the sign for a bunt. Chip stepped up to the third-base side of the plate. Advancing the runners was a must if the Statesmen were going to win this game.

A SUDDEN INSPIRATION

Since Grove was a lefty, anything toward third base would be playing into his hands and provide an easy throw to force out the incoming runner at third base. He noted that Durley and Soapy were poised and ready to take off, but it was evident they were wary of Grove's deadly pickoff talent. Batting righty against Grove's left-hand throws was an asset because it was easier to bunt toward first base. If only he could lay down a slow roller up the first-base path! The Aggies first baseman was edging up toward the grass. Chip closed up his stance a bit.

Grove kept the first pitch high and inside, around his neck. Chip let it go by for a ball. The next pitch was low and inside. Grove wasn't going to give him anything good. Even though a walk would fill the bases, Grove apparently was not too concerned.

Grove's only point in pitching to him, Chip concluded, was that he was a pitcher. The next pitch was shoulder-high. He could have made a try for it, but he let it go for a called strike.

The count was two and one, and he steadied up. Grove now whipped in a curveball that was low, toward Chip's knees. Just before the ball reached the plate, it broke down and started toward the dirt. Chip crouched, stepped toward the ball, and faked the bunt. Then, just as if he had written the script, the ball shot into the dirt and bounced out of the catcher's glove.

The Aggies receiver was on the ball like a cat on a mouse. He made the peg to third, but Durley slid in ahead of the ball. Soapy reached second, and now the tying and winning runs were in scoring position. Chip breathed a sigh of relief and stepped back out of the box.

The stands were hopping. The fans were drumming their feet, applauding, and pleading for a hit. "Bring 'em in, Hilton. Hit away! Win your own game!"

Chip had waited Grove out and forced the count to three and one. The next pitch was a fastball, letter-high and a bit outside. Chip went for it and connected sharply. The ball shot over the Aggies first baseman's head.

Durley broke for the plate, and Soapy headed for third base. The right fielder came in on the dead run, trapped the ball, and fired a strike all the way to the plate. Durley hit the dirt with spikes flashing, but the catcher blocked him away from the plate and tagged him with the ball for the out. Chip rounded first and started toward second, but the catcher had the ball, and he couldn't risk it.

One away!

Crowell dug in at the plate. Chip saw the second baseman edging toward the grass in front of second base at the same time. It was a dead giveaway, and Chip sensed the play before Grove threw to the plate. The pitch was wide, the start of a sucker cutoff play designed to coax Soapy to make a dash for the plate or trap the runner going down to second base. The Aggies catcher got set to make his throw, but Chip made only a false start and then retreated to the bag. Soapy hadn't made a step toward home plate. Ball one!

Burke, coaching in the first-base box, relayed the play. Crowell was on his own. Chip got ready to move, but the pitch to Crowell was low, and the second baseman passed it up. Ball two!

Burke gave him the steal sign, and Chip glanced at the keystone bag guardians. Grove delivered a pitch, and Chip took off for second base. He had the ability to get into full stride quickly and now turned on the steam, watching the Aggies shortstop and second baseman to see which one would take the throw. Both players faked, but neither covered the bag and he went in standing up. The catcher had made no move to make the throw!

The count was two and one, and Crowell, deadly serious, pulled his bat through in several practice swings, determination etched in the expression on his face.

"Watch the pitcher, Chip," Burke called. "I've got the fielders."

Grove delivered, and Crowell took a vicious smash at the ball, sending it on the fly straight into the first baseman's glove. Chip hustled back to second. Two away.

Soapy caught his eye, and Chip read the message as clearly as if the redhead had written him a letter. Soapy wanted to try to steal home. Chip shook his head and pointed toward the next batter, Speed, who was stepping into the batter's box. Speed got set and concentrated on the Aggies pitcher.

Chip checked with Burke and edged toward third base. Speed was a good hitter. The pitch went in, and Speed met the ball cleanly, pulling it over third base. Soapy was off and running. He scored easily. Chip sped toward third.

Malone was looking first at Chip and then at the Aggies left fielder, trying to gauge the distance. Suddenly he began windmilling his arm. Chip circled a bit to the right, turned the corner, stabbed the inside of the bag with his right foot, and sprinted madly for the plate. He could tell from the position of the catcher that the throw was right behind him, and he hit the dirt in a desperate headlong slide with arms outstretched.

Chip's shoulder caught the catcher around the ankles, and he bowled the husky receiver over backward. At the same instant, he heard the ball plunk into the catcher's mitt. He and the Aggies receiver went sprawling over the plate in a tangle of arms and legs. His hand slapped the plate at last, and lying there he saw the ball spin out through the dust and stop just beside the umpire's foot. The catcher had dropped the ball, and he was safe! The Statesmen had come from behind in their last time at bat to pull the game out of the fire. The score: State 9, A & M 8.

Soapy pulled him to his feet, and he was instantly surrounded by his jubilant teammates.

"Great slide, Chip, great!"

"You won the game, kid!"

"And he'll do it again tomorrow!" someone added excitedly.

CHAPTER 9

Helping the Collection Efforts

PORTSIDE HITTERS studded both lineups in Saturday's game the following day. The Aggies manager, Coach Price, started five left-hand batters against Chip Hilton's right-hand pitching, and Coach Rockwell countered with two natural lefties and three switch-hitters to face the visitors' hard-throwing right-handed pitcher. Sitting beside Soapy in the dugout, Chip was thinking that the strategy hadn't helped very much. Neither team had been able to score. A & M star pitcher Ed Crowe had given up only three scratch singles and seemed to be stronger than ever.

"It's pathetic! He's got us eating out of his hand," Soapy muttered. "Look at Gates. Swinging from his heels just like the rest of us."

Chip made no reply. He agreed with Soapy. The Statesmen had better get some runs, and soon. Crowe had handcuffed the State power hitters for six straight innings, and despite the fact that Henry Rockwell had replaced Fireball, Biggie, Red, and Gillen in the bottom of the seventh with new blood, Crowe was still in command.

With the big end of the stick at bat, it should have been State's inning. The fans were standing up for the traditional stretch when the Statesmen came to bat in the bottom of the seventh. They were still on their feet trying to root in some runs as Donovan went down swinging and Green flied out to deep left field.

Burke gave everyone a lift when he bounced the ball over the right-field fence for a ground rule double, but now it looked like he was going to die on second base. Crowe had Gates on the spot with a one-and-two count.

Soapy elbowed Chip. "You've been throwing a lot of fast stuff," the redhead said suggestively.

"I know."

"How about changing things a little? How about concentrating on breaking stuff—curves and sliders against the righty hitters and knucklers and screwballs against the lefties? You could throw the knucklers slow or fast."

"Sounds good."

Crowe's fastball burned in, and Gates lashed at it and missed. Three away!

Chip pulled off his warm-up jacket, picked up his glove, and started for the mound. He glanced at the scoreboard and noted the two long rows of goose eggs. Fourteen big zeros decorated the inning frames of both teams. At the end, under the game summary frames, the Aggies row kept right on going with zeros. The State summary frames showed 0-3-0. No runs! Three hits! No errors!

With the flawless support of his teammates, he hadn't allowed a hit. Soapy had been talking him to death in an effort to conceal the fact. The guys hadn't let on, but Chip knew every one of them was aware of the fact that he had a no-hitter going. They were observing the no-see, no-hear, no-speak tradition, lest they jinx him.

Well, he wasn't going to let it get under his skin. He didn't care how many hits the Aggies got, just so they didn't get any runs!

He got behind on the first Aggies to face him. The hitter batted fifth in the batting order and, while eyeing Chip steadily, waited him out. With the count at two and one, Chip tried to sneak a curveball across the outside corner, but the ball had too much stuff on it and went spinning too far to the outside. Three and one! Now he *had* to come in there . . . and the hitter knew it too!

He fired his fastball, and the batter watched it go by for strike two. Soapy called for another curveball, but Chip kept looking at the redhead until he got the sign for a fastball. Chip knew that no good pitcher would take a chance on walking the first man up. He came in with his heater and the batter pickled it.

C-r-a-c-k!

The ball was a blur of white close to the ground on his right. Without thinking of the consequences, he went for it with his right hand. He didn't catch the ball, but he did knock it down. Durley came in on the dead run and pounced on it. His lightning throw to Green just barely beat the runner. It was a big break! Now, instead of a runner on first with hitters coming up to send him around, there was one away and no one on.

His fingers were numb, and he massaged them gently as the ball went around the horn and in to Soapy. The redhead walked slowly out to the mound. "All right?" he asked anxiously. Chip nodded. After a second, Soapy handed the ball to him and went back to the plate.

Chip's fingers were still tingling when he pitched to the next batter. The result was his second walk of the game and one away with a man on first. Chip considered the situation. Batting seventh, the next batter could be any kind of a hitter. He would pitch to him and have to be ready for anything.

It was easy. He struck him out with two wide curveballs and a fastball to the inside. Two away!

The catcher was up. Like many catchers, he was a husky player with broad shoulders and piano legs. He had grounded out the first time at bat, and Chip had struck him out the last time. For some reason, the batter reminded Chip of Ben Green, and he decided to keep the ball low. It was the ticket! He struck out the receiver again with two fastballs kept low and away from the hitter and a screwball. It was time to get some runs!

It was the bottom of the eighth, and the small end of the stick was up. Durley led off with Soapy in the on-deck circle. Crowe had the stocky, hot-corner star's number and made him hit one on the ground, an easy out from the second baseman to catch him at first. One away.

As Soapy went up to the plate, Chip took his own favorite bat and the warm-up bat and walked out to the on-deck circle. The redhead was determined to get on, but Crowe didn't intend to walk him. He showed Soapy a variety of breaking pitches, low and inside, low and outside, and one that dropped down a foot. Soapy went for all three of them and struck out. Two away.

The fans gave Chip a round of applause when he stepped into the left side of the batting box. He took his time getting set and tried to still the wild pounding of his heart. With two away and no need to check the signs, he was completely on his own. There was nothing to do but hit the ball. He pulled his bat through in a smooth swing and concentrated on Crowe's motion.

The Aggies was a hard-nosed hurler, a real competitor, and he had been keeping ahead of the State hitters all through the game. The three previous times Chip had come to bat, he had looked Crowe's pitches over until the umpire called a strike. He made up his mind to lay into the very first pitch—*if* Crowe grooved it down the middle.

Sure enough, the hurler drilled it right down the middle. Chip concentrated on just meeting the ball, but he must have put his weight into the swing. The ball took off on a straight line for the right-field fence, soared over the wire and across the street, and landed on someone's lawn. The home-run kids took off after the ball with wild yells of joy. *This* was how he preferred to help their collection efforts!

The blow brought the fans to their feet en masse. They were still standing and yelling and stomping when he trotted around third and in to the plate. Practically the entire State University team was waiting to slap him on the back; his teammates surrounded him on the way to the dugout.

Just as he ducked down under the shelter, he caught Ben Green's eye. Big Ben's face expressed mixed emotions: part joy, part disappointment, and maybe a bit of jealousy, it seemed to Chip. Green quickly turned away.

The State fans wanted some more runs and were still yelling when Crowell came to bat, but Crowe struck him out with three straight breaking balls to retire the side. Chip gave his teammates a chance to get out on the field and took his time walking to the mound.

The three zeros remained in the Aggies summary, but the State frames now showed 1-4-0. One run. Four hits. No errors. Three *big* outs to go.

The Aggies coach sent in a lefty pinch hitter for pitcher Ed Crowe, and Chip struck him out with two slow curves and a blazing slider. One away!

The Statesmen were pepping it up now, and Chip took a quick look around. With the exception of Green on first base, the infield lineup was the same that had started the game. It seemed strange, however, not to see Red in left or Fireball in center field.

The leadoff hitter was up, and Chip remembered that he had grounded out, walked, and flied out to Fireball. Since the Aggies coach had left him in the game, it meant the third baseman was a strong batter. Chip pitched carefully, and the count went to three and two. Soapy called for a change-up, and the batter fanned. Two away!

He took a deep breath and turned once more to look at his teammates. Then he heard the fans. It was a buzzing sound at first, like a lot of bees. The buzzing grew and grew until it seemed to Chip that every person in the stands was yelling all at once. A fan shouted, "No-hitter," and another echoed the cry. Others joined in and the cry became a chant: "No-hitter! No-hitter! No-hitter!"

Soapy hurried his sign for a breaking ball, but Chip kept peering in at him until the redhead changed his call to a fastball. Chip nodded. He wanted to get this over with in a hurry.

He put his back into his fastball, and the batter met it right on the nose. The ball headed toward left field, and Chip felt sure it was in there. Before he could turn to look, he heard a tremendous shout from the stands and turned just in time to see Speed fully extended, hanging in the air, it seemed, with the ball buried in his glove.

The game was over! State had made it two in a row over the Aggies, and he had pitched a no-hitter! It was a storybook finish.

CHAPTER 10

The Home-Run Kids

SOAPY SMITH had the Sunday papers spread all over their dorm room: on the beds, on his desk, and on the floor. Holding up a sheaf of clippings, he shook them toward Chip. "These are the Saturday clippings," he said. "You want to see them?"

Chip had been trying to study, but he hadn't made much progress. Soapy had kept up a steady chatter, describing each article as he cut it out of the paper. He looked up and shook his head. "No, Soapy," he said, somewhat annoyed, "I don't. I was *trying* to study."

"You oughta look at this one," Soapy said sweetly, handing the top clipping to Chip. "It's about Ben Green."

BEN GREEN SEEKS STATE HOME-RUN MARK

Former high school star Ben Green yesterday initiated his State baseball career with a three-run homer. The big first baseman says his ambition is to break the home-run record he set in junior college when he smacked out sixteen round-trippers in a twenty-game schedule.

Green has the body and muscle to do it. He carries a long, thirty-six-ounce bat up to the plate, and he handles the club as if it were a matchstick.

The local belter is counting on his power at the plate to win him a starting spot on the varsity.

"Well?" Soapy asked, waiting for Chip's reaction.

"There's nothing wrong with that," Chip answered.

Soapy dug into the Sunday stack of clippings. "All right," he said excitedly, happy Chip was finally looking at clippings with him. "Tell me what's wrong with this one!"

"All right," Chip said in mock resignation. "Let's see it."

THE NAME OF THE GAME IS PITCHING
State's Hilton Wins Pitching Duel

All-American pitching star Chip Hilton, State's captain and star pitcher, yesterday combined a brilliant no-hitter with an eighth-inning home run to personally account for the 1-0 defeat of arch rival A & M. It was a one-man show.

The blond bomber struck out sixteen men in the pitchers' duel, but the star was full of praise for the support of his teammates and gave them full credit for the no-hitter.

Be that as it may, the hitting of the long-ball sluggers, which was supposed to be the team's forte, was disappointing and conspicuous by its absence. Hilton got two of the Statesmen's four hits.

The luckless loser in this dramatic one-man exhibition was A & M's number-one pitcher, Ed Crowe. The Aggies hurler struck out fourteen Statesmen and limited them to four hits, all singles with the exception of Hilton's game-winning home-run blast.

> The two-day series points out in no uncertain terms the limited pitching staff with which Coach Henry Rockwell must defend State's conference and national titles. Hilton can work every three or four days, but there are five weekend two-game series included in the schedule as well as four instances of three-games-in-four-days stints to contend with.

"Pretty good, eh?" Soapy demanded.

Chip shook his head. "No, it isn't. The fact that we won is great, but all that stuff about a one-man show and the no-hitter and the home run isn't fair to the rest of the team. Nor to me. It could upset the whole team." He paused and thought about it for a moment and then continued. "The team is everything. People don't care what Chip Hilton does as an individual."

Chip soon found that he had erred in thinking people didn't care what he did as an individual. On the way to church, he met a crowd of boys and girls coming home from Sunday school. The youngsters surrounded him as if he had pitched a no-hitter in the World Series. He answered all their questions and signed autographs until they continued on down the street. Then he sighed in relief and continued on to church.

The adulation didn't end with the youngsters. It was the same all day: in church, on University's streets, and at Grayson's. He was glad when it was time to go home to Jeff.

Monday morning it was worse. The campus was alive with baseball talk, and he was right in the middle of the whole thing, starting at breakfast in the student union. Classmates and professors stopped by his usual breakfast table to congratulate him. It was great for a player's ego, but he didn't like this sort of foolishness. Sure, it was great to pitch a no-hitter. He was proud of the feat, but the team had won the game, not Chip Hilton!

Classes went quickly, and Chip was pleased to escape the attention of the day when he and Soapy started out for practice. Hopefully, now all the adulation would be forgotten. As he and Soapy approached Alumni Field, they saw a group of youngsters standing in front of the bleachers gate. The middle school boys were huddled in a close knot, gesturing and talking loudly, apparently engaged in some sort of a game.

One of the boys broke out of the circle, stubbornly shaking his head. Then he saw Chip and Soapy and immediately turned back. Pointing toward them, he said something to his friends. As if on signal, the boys turned swiftly and pressed forward. They waited quietly enough, but Chip noticed they were eyeing him appraisingly.

They were close to the group now, and the boy who had first spotted him took a step forward. "You're Chip Hilton, aren't you?" he asked, looking at Chip.

"Yes, I am. What's your name?"

"Mark. Mark Parsons. You're captain of the State baseball team, right?"

Chip nodded. "That's right."

The little guy's eyes were sparkling as he turned back to the others. "I knew it," he said proudly.

Facing Chip again, he continued the interrogation. "Didn't you pitch the no-hitter yesterday?"

"He sure did!" Soapy broke in, his blue eyes flashing.

"Are you on the team too?" Mark asked.

Soapy nodded vigorously. "I sure am! I'm a catcher, Chip's battery mate in fact."

"Didn't you play last year when Hilton was pitching and the team won the national championship?"

"I sure did! He's going to do it again too. We're going to make it two in a row."

"It's never been done," Chip added, "but it's our big dream."

"You'll do it," Mark said confidently. "You made all-American pitcher last year, didn't you?"

"That didn't have anything to do with winning the championship."

"Yes, it did!" Mark said quickly. "That's what we've been arguing about. My dad really knows baseball, and he says it takes pitchers to win and they—" Mark stopped and gestured over his shoulder toward the others. "They say it takes sluggers, home-run hitters."

There was a murmur of assent from the group as a tall, heavy-set boy moved up beside Mark and elbowed him roughly aside. His mouth was full of chewing gum. "We're right too!" he said, looking contemptuously at Mark. "You can't win games without runs, and the only way to get them is to hit the ball."

The resemblance to Ben Green was so pronounced that it seemed foolish to ask the chubby youngster his name, but Chip did it anyway. "Your name is—"

"Marty Green," the boy said boldly. "My brother is the best ballplayer in town. It says so right here in the paper. Look!"

Chip glanced at the clipping's headline. "BEN GREEN SEEKS STATE HOME-RUN MARK." It was the one from the *Herald* that Soapy had shown him. Chip nodded and smiled. "I saw it," he said gently. "Your brother is a great hitter, Marty, but it takes a team to win games and championships. It isn't all pitching and—"

"I'll say it ain't," a loud, voice interrupted sarcastically. Ben Green had approached unheard, but Chip knew his voice. He turned around, but before he could speak, Marty beat him to it. "Ben!" the boy cried delightedly. "You got here just in time." He hooked a thumb toward Chip. "He says—"

"I know, I know," Green interrupted. "Hilton says pitching wins the games. Well, bein' a pitcher, he would. But anyone with an ounce of sense knows it's the hitters who win the games . . . and the championships! That's not all either," he added quickly, looking straight at Chip. "Hitters have been known to make all-Americans out of some college pitchers."

Marty was grinning broadly. "I told you!" he said triumphantly, turning to the other boys. "I was right!"

"It doesn't make it right just because your brother says so," Mark observed sourly.

"Does too!"

Ben took it from there. "Marty's right," he said belligerently. "Where would the Yankees have been without home-run hitters? They've been world champions more often than any team in baseball. Who do you think was responsible for that, the pitchers? That's a laugh! Babe Ruth and Lou Gehrig and Joe DiMaggio and Yogi Berra and Roger Maris and Mickey Mantle and Don Mattingly and 'Mr. October,' Reggie Jackson, and Derek Jeter—hitters like *that* won the pennants."

"If I remember my baseball history, Berra and Mantle and Maris didn't do so much back in 1963," Soapy countered quickly. "As I recall, the Yankees got only four runs in four games and only one home run! The Dodgers pitchers, Koufax, Podres, and Drysdale, beat 'em four straight games in the World Series. Besides, the World Series is full of examples of great players, but it takes a team working together to win it all."

Green eyed Soapy with tolerant disdain. "Huh!" he said shortly. "A lot you know about hitting. Big-league managers take ballplayers who can't hit and make pitchers out of them." He paused and waved a hand at the redhead. "If you know so much, Smith, suppose you name a pitcher who can hit."

"Chip can hit! Rock used him in the cleanup spot lots of times last year."

"Huh!" Green cried contemptuously. "Hilton is Rockwell's wonder boy. He puts him in all the glory spots, but that doesn't make him a cleanup hitter."

"He won the game Saturday with a home run."

A surge of anger had gripped Chip and stayed with him. Green's reference to hitters making all-Americans of some college pitchers really bothered him. For a moment his emotions got the best of him, and all he could think of was a showdown. Then he remembered the home-run kids and forced down the urge to lash back. Holding himself in check, he managed to speak calmly. "Coach Rockwell's never played favorites in his life."

Green looked at the group of boys to make sure he had their full attention. They were watching him closely as he turned back to Chip. "No? Then get this! Rockwell and Bill Bell and Jim Locke are all alike. Bill Bell puts your name in the *Herald* every day, and Jim Locke is just as bad. He oughta change the name of the *News* to the *Chip Hilton Daily*."

The home-run kids were absorbed in the argument and drinking in every word. Hooking his thumb toward them, Green continued his tirade, "Now it's the kids. The papers have got them believing all a ball club needs is a pitcher and a baseball. Some nonsense that is! A bunch of hitters knock in seven or eight runs, and then the pitcher gets credit for winning the game."

"The scoreboard numbers are a convenience to pitchers, but no one believes pitchers win games when runs are scored." Chip answered calmly. "I know as well as anybody that hitters always get the runs."

"Of course they do! They win the pennants in the big leagues too! Before this season is over, Bill Bell and Jim Locke will be eatin' crow, or my name isn't Ben Green. All they ever write about is you and your pitching. It's about time a couple of hitters got their names in the papers."

"You're welcome to all the publicity as far as I'm concerned," Chip said evenly, turning away.

"I'll get it!" Green boasted.

"Good luck," Chip called over his shoulder. He and Soapy walked on, leaving Green talking to his brother. Mark Parsons and several of the smaller boys moved away from the other youngsters and followed.

"Hey! Chip Hilton," Mark called, "How about your autograph?"

Chip and Soapy waited for the boys to catch up. Mark dug into his pocket and came out with a handful of cards. "Baseball bubble gum cards," he explained. "We trade them. I'm a pitcher like you, so I save cards of pitchers. One day I hope to get a Sandy Koufax card." He held out three cards with the pictures of baseball players printed on them. "Orel Hershiser, Nolan Ryan, and Roger Clemens!" he announced proudly. "You can sign all three of them on the back."

"I save catchers," one of the other boys volunteered. "I think the catcher is the smartest player on the team. I've even got a Johnny Bench card at home, but my dad said it better not leave the house."

"You're so right about catchers," Soapy said, beaming proudly. "You gotta be pretty smart to be a catcher."

"I know," the boy said confidently. "I'm a catcher too."

"Are you the guys who patrol the fences for home-run balls every afternoon?" Chip asked.

"That's us! But we're not there every afternoon," Mark said. "We made up our own league, and it takes most of our time. We come to all your games though."

"We've got some tough competition in our league," the catcher said ruefully. "Besides, we have trouble getting good baseballs to practice with. Marty and the big guys get most of them."

"Where do you play your games?" Chip asked.

"You know where the college teachers park their cars?" Mark asked.

Chip nodded. "That's only a block from Jeff, where we live."

"Well, that's where we play our games. It's not much of a field, but it's better than no field at all."

"Some of the bigger guys play ball there at night," the catcher added.

"What about lights?" Soapy asked.

"The parking lot light is OK," the catcher explained helpfully.

Mark nodded in agreement. "That's right." He shook his head and added quickly, "We don't play at night though. We aren't allowed out that late."

"Marty Green does," the catcher volunteered. "He plays first base, just like his brother."

"The older guys are pretty tough," another boy ventured.

"Yes, and they're going to get in trouble one of these days," Mark added soberly.

"Stay away from them," Chip advised.

"We do, except when we need baseballs," Mark said. "Then we have to take our chances outside the ball-park fence."

"We get one or two a week," the catcher said. "The big guys are older and tougher, but we're faster."

"Baseball is a game of speed," Soapy said quickly. "Run 'em ragged!"

"They chase us ragged after we grab a homer," Mark said, grinning.

Chip and Soapy signed a few more cards and continued on toward the grandstand. Soapy had been pleasant enough with the kids, but Chip knew that underneath, the redhead was burning with anger. His freckles stood out in sharp relief against his flushed face, and he bit his words off savagely when they were alone.

"Green's been ridin' you long enough," Soapy fumed. "You're a better hitter than he'll ever be. Now he's trying to sell his home-run garbage to the kids. He'll have them trying to do the same thing—trying to kill the ball every time they swing a bat."

"Maybe, but you can't fool kids, Soapy."

"He can."

"I doubt it."

Soapy shook his head stubbornly. "You'll see. Anyway, he's jealous of you, so jealous it hurts."

"I don't see why."

"Are you kidding? Look! You're the first three-sport all-American in State's history, right?"

Chip shrugged. "I really don't know what that has to do with Green, Soapy."

"Nonsense! It happens to be a simple fact. You're also getting a lot of publicity in the local papers. You agree to that, don't you?"

"But why the jealousy?" Chip prodded.

"Why? Because Green's been the big local star for years. He was the hero all through high school."

"And—"

"And he doesn't like competition," the redhead finished.

"That doesn't make sense. He plays first base and I pitch."

"All right then," Soapy said in resignation. "I'll spell it out for you slowly. When Green got through high school, his grades weren't good enough to get him into State. So he had to go to a junior college for a couple of years to get the credits to get him into State. Well, he got the credits, and now he's here, and he's out to prove he's everything his hometown thinks he is."

"So he's good. What has that got to do with me?"

"Everything! As I said before, you happen to be big sports news all over the country, and he can't take it. He was the big local hero until you came along, and now he's green with envy. Hey! That's good—green with envy. It sticks out on him like the nose on his mean, sloppy face."

"Or like Soapy Smith's freckles," Chip added teasingly.

Soapy didn't think that was funny and made a face to show it. He took the lead and strode swiftly and purposefully through the players' entrance and down the steps to the locker room, his head held high. "Leave my freckles out of this!" he chirped good-naturedly. "Let's go play some ball and show everyone what this team can do."

CHAPTER 11

Busts
Wide Open

CHIP FOLLOWED Soapy into the locker room and landed
smack in the middle of a heated argument. Andre Durley
and Darrin Nickels were really going at it. The rest of the
players were in front of their lockers putting on their uniforms or lacing up their spikes or talking softly among themselves, pretending not to hear, but they all knew what was
going on. Out of the corners of their eyes all were watching
the burly catcher and the fiery little third baseman and listening closely to their conversation.

"I'll say it again!" Durley shouted, banging his locker
door. "Good pitching and tight defense won the championship for us last year."

"What about Cohen and Finley?" Nickels countered. "And
Burke and Engle? They were on the team too. Didn't their
hitting help win the championship?"

"Of course!" Durley answered irritably. "That's not what
I'm getting at. I'm not talking about ability. I'm talking
about team play, about *inside* baseball. Last year we had it.
We worked on it in practice and among ourselves, and we

used it in the games. This year there's no inside baseball. Every player on the team wants to be a home-run slugger."

"Including the pitchers," Gillen called out pointedly. The remark could have been friendly or antagonistic. Chip chose to regard it as a joke and smiled. Then he remembered Diz Dean's curt manner when he had relieved the big lefty in the first Aggies game. He glanced at Dean just in time to catch his eye. The pitcher's gaze wavered, and a faint flush swept across his face as he turned his head away.

"It doesn't make any difference who it is," Durley said stubbornly. "It's the big reason we're not getting runs."

"How do you get runs if you don't hit?" Engle asked sarcastically.

"I didn't say we shouldn't hit," Andre corrected him. "I said we ought to try to get someone on base before we try to *kill* the ball. If we can get a runner on first, then the hitters can send him on around."

"So tell us, great wise one, how are we going to get on base if we don't hit the ball?" Dean taunted, snickering.

"By making the pitcher work! By looking 'em over, by trying to make him give you a walk, by dragging a bunt, and by passing up every pitch that doesn't come into the strike zone. *That's* how!"

"OK, so we get someone on first," Nickels said. "Then what?"

"We advance him to second," Durley explained. "We use the bunt or the hit-and-run. That way, if we do it right, we keep away from double plays. First we get a man in scoring position; *then* we go for the big hit."

"Andre is right on!" Crowell called out over his shoulder.

"Of course you'd think that," Nickels said sarcastically. "All you infielders *ever* do is bunt."

"That's because they can't hit the ball over the fence," Al Engle chirped.

Speed couldn't stand for that. "I didn't see *you* knock anything over the fence on Friday," he said.

"Right!" Engle agreed, nodding. "How about you?"

"Speed knocked in the two runs that won the game," Schwartz said angrily.

There was a tight silence, and Chip could feel the tension growing in the room. Then Ben Green elbowed his way into the discussion. Ben had come into the locker room while Andre Durley was speaking, and Chip knew the big player had waited to hear enough to fill himself in before he spoke up. Green was ready now, and the lull gave him a chance.

"That stuff you're spouting is just garbage, Andre," Green said loudly. "Most of the *real* ballplayers on this ball club go for the power game."

"Right!" Gillen said.

"Amen," Nickels added.

Biggie, Fireball, and Burke didn't say anything, but out of the corner of his eye, Chip saw them nod their heads in approval. He couldn't blame them. The greatest thrill in the game was hitting a home run.

"The only reason we haven't hit our stride," Green explained, "is because pitchers are always ahead of batters early in the season. Any day now we're going to open up with the greatest barrage of home runs since McGwire and Sosa. We'll be like the old-timers who did it: Ruth, Gehrig, Lazzeri, and Dickey!"

"Give me a break!" Jerry Gold said with disgust.

Murph Kelly had been quietly going about organizing the first-aid kit. He looked around the room now and snorted. "Why don't you clubhouse lawyers go out on the field where you belong? I need some breathing space. You guys win a couple of games and begin acting like national champions."

"We *are* national champions," Soapy yelped.

"History! That was last year!" Kelly retorted, frowning deeply.

Chip, troubled, finished lacing up his spikes and jogged out to the field. Something was building up, and it wasn't good! More than just a difference of opinions had emerged in the locker room. Chip had felt a mild undercurrent of resentment toward himself, and he knew the big write-ups in the Sunday papers were responsible—as if he had anything to do with the sportswriters and what they wrote in their news stories.

Bill Bell and Jim Locke were friendly, and he figured he could ask them to ease up on writing about his pitching. Hopefully that would take care of the publicity problem. He didn't know what he could do about the cliques.

He ran over the names of those who had taken sides in the argument. Engle, Nickels, Gillen, and Dean always supported one another. Green had joined up on their side, and Davis and Foster would go along with him. Chip knew that where Dean went, he would find Sparks. That added up to eight.

On the other side of the fence were Durley, Crowell, Speed, Dugan, Schwartz, and Soapy. Gold had surprised him by siding with Durley. Where Gold went, he would find Donovan and Gates, and that added up to nine.

Biggie, Fireball, and Burke hadn't expressed much interest either way, but Chip knew they favored the power game. That left him all alone and smack in the middle. As captain of the team, he couldn't favor either side.

He took his laps and joined the pepper game that Durley and Crowell were staging near third base. Over on the other side of the field, the long-ball hitters were having a great time with the same warm-up practice. Burke, Gillen, Green, Engle, Dean, Nickels, and Cohen were in this group.

Coach Rockwell and his assistant, Bill Malone, appeared on the field, and that broke up the pepper games as practice began. The coaches sent them through some baserunning and a long batting practice.

During batting practice, all the power hitters were straining for the fences. Rockwell watched them for a time and then called for a stop to the overswinging, but it didn't do much good. They toned down their efforts for a round and then went right back to taking vicious cuts at the ball, trying to outdo one another and knock the cover off the apple. When they didn't hit a long ball, they changed their stances, moving to the front or the rear of the box and closer to the plate or away from it.

Rockwell again called a halt to the heavy hitting. This time he summoned the entire squad to home plate and gave everyone a going-over. Then, after a snappy fielding practice, he told them to take two laps and hit the showers.

Chip challenged Speed and Fireball to a race, and they took off. Fireball kept up until they were halfway around on their second lap. Then Chip and Speed stepped up the pace until they were sprinting at full speed. Fireball was slowly left behind. It was a close race between the two friends, and every player on the field kept an eye on the result. Chip and Speed had raced this way for years—ever since their elementary school days back in Valley Falls. They were neck and neck until thirty feet from home plate. Then Chip's long strides began to tell. He inched his way ahead to win by a stride.

Tuesday afternoon's practice brought more batting surprises. The power hitters showed up at practice with all kinds of bats: long, fat, heavy, light, wooden, aluminum, some with short handles, some with long handles, and even one plastic wiffle bat. It would have been funny, Chip was thinking, except that it represented the home-run fever that now gripped the Statesmen. Anyway, he reflected, the locker room discussions had been a little lighter and were now focused on the array of bats instead of heated arguments.

Out on the field, Rockwell put them through a short, snappy workout and then called everyone in for a conference in front of the dugout. "We take our first road trip tomorrow," he said, "and the bus leaves from in front of Assembly Hall at nine o'clock sharp. Be there!

"We should arrive back here late Sunday afternoon. Bring your books and plan to do some studying. Dean Murray told me some of you are slacking off. That reminds me—don't miss any classes. You all know the absence rule. An athletic absence counts one-third, but a regular absence counts a full point. Remember, and *this is important:* Your total number of absences govern your eligibility. If you are absent as much as one-third of a class more than the total number of semester hours on your program, you are automatically out of athletics. There's no recourse. You're through for the year!

"The three games coming up this week mean a lot. Three wins would put us at the top in the conference standings. Let's get a good night's rest. We're going to come back here Sunday undefeated and leading the league!"

"We'll *kill* 'em!" Soapy growled, thumping Chip and Speed on their backs.

Late Sunday afternoon, five days later, Chip was stretched out on his bed relaxing in Jefferson Hall, thinking back to the events of the road trip. Soapy was sitting on the floor, cutting stories out of the *News* and the *Herald* and reading aloud the glowing tributes paid to the Statesmen.

At the end of Tuesday's practice, Soapy had said, "We'll kill 'em," and the Statesmen had done just that. State University had made a sweep of all three games.

Ben Green had been right too. The Statesmen had burst out with a barrage of home runs.

Rockwell's prophesy had come true to the letter. State had returned undefeated and leading the league.

Chip had pitched the Wednesday and Saturday games. Wesleyan was a weak-hitting team and was plagued by poor pitching. The Statesmen bunched their hits at the right time and knocked three pitchers out of the box. Chip had pitched a shutout on Wednesday, winning 14-0. It had been that easy.

The power hitters had kept up their slugging ways on Friday against Southern, and Rockwell had caught Diz Dean on one of his better days. The unpredictable lefty was wild, but he finished the game on the mound. Both teams had hit the ball solidly, but State had the better defense and won a close game. The score: State 9, Southern 7.

Chip had pitched again on Saturday. The guys had hit the ball at the right time and made the game a winner. It was the first time Chip had felt tired, but there was too much at stake to risk losing the game. He had called on every bit of his reserve strength and managed to ride it out. The State University Statesmen had made it a twin killing over Southern, running their victory streak to five in a row. The score: State 7, Southern 5.

Soapy interrupted his thoughts. "Look at that spread!" he said with pride, holding up the sports page of the *Herald*. "Did you read it?"

Chip shook his head. "Nope."

"Well, you'd better! It's either awfully good or awfully bad, I don't know which."

"What do you mean?" Chip asked, getting up from his bed.

"Here," Soapy explained, handing the paper to Chip, "have a look."

STATE BOMBERS EXPLODE SIXTEEN HOMERS
IN THREE ROAD GAMES

State's long-ball bombers went on a three-game record-breaking spree this past week when they blasted sixteen home runs and defeated Wesleyan (once) and Southern (twice). No less than seven Statesmen took part in the home-run slaughter of their conference rivals.

Biggie Cohen, veteran first baseman, led the bombing with four home runs, blasting three of them on Friday against Southern.

Belter Burke and University's own Ben Green tied with three homers each, Finley and Engle with two each, and Hilton and Nickels with one each.

What is most certainly a conference record occurred on Friday in the first Southern game when the State fence busters hammered out nine home runs. The major-league mark stands at eight, which is a good indicator of the magnitude of the Statesmen's feat.

Two games are on tap during the coming week, Western at home on Wednesday and Eastern away on Saturday.

"Well," Soapy said, when Chip finished reading the story, "is it good or bad?"

"It's always good when you win," Chip responded.

Soapy's eyes narrowed. "You know what I mean. Answer the question."

"If you mean, does it add fuel to the home-run race, I say yes. Ben Green always did swing from his heels. Now Biggie and the rest of the guys are doing the same thing."

"How come Rock keeps alternating Biggie and Ben Green? Biggie makes Ben look like a beginner."

"Ben can't play anywhere but at first base, Soapy. If Rock doesn't give him a chance to play, the second-guessers in this town will be after Coach's scalp. You know that."

"Well," Soapy sighed, biting his lip and shaking his head, "I told you a long time ago that Ben Green spelled trouble. You'll see. He's got a feud going, and he isn't going to be satisfied until he gets everyone thinking his way."

Responding to Chip's calm expression, Soapy continued, "I mean it! Mark my words! He's going to keep on until this team busts wide open."

"Maybe not."

"You'll see. I guess you heard what Murphy Gillen said right after the Saturday game."

Chip nodded and buried his nose in the paper. He had heard Gillen loud and clear. He could still hear his teammate's words: "This isn't a one-man show! The *hitters* won this game and the others too!"

CHAPTER 12

Power of the Press

SOAPY SMITH was leading the way through the players' exit to the field. Without warning, he stopped so quickly that Chip nearly ran into him. "Look at that!" the redhead managed, pointing and turning his head toward the field.

Chip stepped forward and couldn't believe his eyes. The grandstand and bleachers were jammed with spectators, and several sportswriters and photographers were talking to the players out on the diamond.

Bill Bell, sports editor of the *Herald,* was talking to Coach Henry Rockwell in front of the home dugout. On the other side of the field, Jim Locke, the senior writer for the *News,* was busy lining up Cohen, Green, Burke, Finley, Engle, and Nickels in front of the visitors' dugout.

Someone must have seen Chip coming out to the field and advised the sportswriter because Locke turned swiftly and waved. "Hey, Hilton!" he called, windmilling an arm. "Come over here and get in the picture."

"Oh, no!" Chip groaned, glancing at Soapy.

"You've got to go," Soapy warned. "You know the power of the press."

The redhead trotted off, and Chip walked over to join the group. Locke extended his hand and led him toward the dugout. "We've been waiting for you," he explained. "I want to get a picture of all the players who hit those home runs last week."

"You don't want me," Chip said, laughing. "I'm a pitcher."

"You've got that right, Hilton! Who needs pitchers when State's got hitters like us?" Ben Green chortled gleefully. "We're operating under a new system, Durley or no Durley. We're just gonna knock in more runs than the other team. We don't care how many runs they get. We'll get more!"

"That's the idea of the game," Nickels said significantly. "You can't win without runs."

"Or *get* runs without hits," Engle added.

Locke was placing the players where he wanted them for the camera, but he was aware of the trend of the conversation. He stopped and held up his hand. "I guess I owe you men an apology. It was a rough going-over a week ago. Yesterday I reversed my stance and praised you to the skies. Anyway, you've got the best pitcher and the greatest long-ball bombers in college baseball right here."

"Yeah," Green said, "but we've got an argument going. Me and the rest of the home-run hitters say a team wins pennants by knocking the ball crazy. Hilton and Durley and the bunters say pitching and defense wins. What do you think?"

"Oh, no, Ben," Locke said, laughing. "You're not putting me on *that* spot! You guys have to battle that one out on your own."

The sportswriter placed Chip in the center of the group and focused his camera. "All right, now," he said, "hold it! Let's get this over with." He snapped the camera and held them for a second shot before the group broke up.

Chip started out to take his laps, but Locke called out to him. "Wait a minute, Hilton," he said. "I want to get a picture of you for a story I'm writing about no-hitters."

It was the break Chip had hoped for. He posed for the picture and then told Locke about the feelings that had developed on the team because of the no-hitter publicity.

Locke listened attentively and then shook his head. "You're wrong, Hilton, dead wrong. A reporter has to give credit where it's due. Take yesterday's stories. The credit went to the hitters, probably the same players who were griping because *you* got big coverage last week. Forget it! Everything evens up in the long run. You just keep sending that fastball of yours past the hitters and let the chips fall where they may."

Chip thanked Locke and took his laps. On the way around the field, he thought it over. Now he knew just how his teammates were lined up. Biggie, Fireball, and Burke weren't going to join either group. They were strong, unafraid, confident, and not about to get trapped into *any* situation that would hurt the team.

Well, Chip concluded, he would pitch his heart out, stay out of the arguments, take Green's insults, and hope for the best. He said a silent prayer for patience as he loped around the field.

Western arrived in University to face the Statesmen on Wednesday, and Chip was on the mound when the game began. He had never felt better. Nor could he ever remember when his fastball had experienced a better hop. When he sidearmed the ball, his curves were breaking as wide as a door. When he threw an overhand curve, it broke down as if it had fallen off a table. He had the Westerners spooked all through the game. Biggie, Green, and Burke each added one more round-tripper to their personal totals.

Although Chip's arm was tired when he walked off the mound at the end of the game, he felt wonderful. He had pitched his second shutout, and the Statesmen had won their fifth game of the season. He looked over his shoulder at the scoreboard: State 9, Visitors 0.

The Statesmen had won six straight games and were in undisputed possession of first place in the conference.

On Thursday and Friday the team practices were routine. There was still some talk in the locker room over the pitching versus hitting controversy, but recently the newspapers had focused on the hitters, which left them with little to gripe about.

Ben Green, however, was the exception. Chip was convinced that Green's griping was habit more than anything else. At any rate, Green had quieted down a bit. Coach Rockwell was dividing the first-base job between Biggie and the rabble-rouser, and Chip figured that accounted for the change.

The home-run kids were absent during practice, but when Chip and Soapy walked out of the players' gate after the workout, Mark and the little catcher were waiting for them.

"What are you guys doing here?" Chip asked. "It's late. You ought to be home."

"It's all right," Mark assured them. "We're a committee, and we're on a mission. We want to ask you something."

"A committee?" Soapy echoed, grinning at Chip.

"Yep! Our manager sent us to ask you to give us a clinic next Sunday afternoon. Will you do it?"

"It would be a big thing for Mark and me," the catcher added.

"Where?"

"You know," Mark said, "next to the college parking lot."

"What time?"

"Any time in the afternoon."

"Four o'clock?"

"That's great!"

"All right, Soapy and I will be there. We might bring some friends too. Baseball players. All right?"

"Wow! Yes!"

"Good enough. We'll see you Sunday afternoon."

Chip and Soapy lost no time getting down to Grayson's. Friday night was one of the busiest nights of the week, and it seemed as if every baseball fan in town came in at one time or another on this particular evening. Soapy and Fireball and the rest of the fountain crew were kept hopping all evening.

Chip was glad when it was time to close up. He secured the stockroom and walked out to the front of the store where Soapy was waiting. Biggie Cohen was with him.

"Hey!" Chip said in surprise. "You're out late, aren't you?"

"A little," Biggie said, laughing. "I've got a good excuse though. Abe's outside. He's up here for a ceramics convention. He'll be here several days. After I drop him off at the hotel, I'll drive you home. All the meetings are in the hotel, so Abe said I could use his new car while he's here."

"Come on, Chip," Soapy said eagerly, "let's go see Abe."

Outside, parked at the curb, was a shiny, red car. "Wow!" Soapy cried. "Have we got color!"

Abe Cohen was Biggie's oldest brother. He was seated in the rear seat, and Speed Morris was in the front. Chip and Soapy piled in beside Abe in the back seat, glad to see their old friend. Biggie took the wheel. On the way to the Holiday Inn, Abe filled them in on the Valley Falls news. Biggie dropped his brother off at the hotel and drove on toward Jeff.

"Where you gonna park?" Soapy asked. "You can't leave a car on the street, and you don't have a parking sticker for the college. College security has been handin' out tickets right and left."

"I know," Biggie said. "I went over to security this afternoon and asked them where to park. They told me to put it in the faculty parking lot. There's lots of room there at night."

"We'll go with you," Chip said.

Biggie parked the car, and Chip located the baseball field Mark had described. It wasn't much of a field, but as Mark had said, it was better than nothing at all.

They walked slowly back to Jefferson Hall, talking about Abe and Valley Falls. Biggie promised to pick them up in Abe's car at the store at twelve the next day and drive them to Alumni Field. When they reached the dorm, Biggie and Speed joined some of the guys watching a movie in the first-floor lounge, but Chip and Soapy went on upstairs to their room. Half an hour later they were in bed and sound asleep.

Soapy beat the alarm by a second the next morning and slipped out of the room moments later. When he came back with hot chocolate and doughnuts, and the morning papers tucked under his arm, Chip was dressed and ready to start for Grayson's. They walked briskly to the store and went to work. The morning passed quickly. Just before noon, Chip joined Soapy and Fireball at the fountain for a sandwich and a glass of milk. At exactly twelve o'clock, Biggie arrived and drove them to Alumni Field.

The grandstand was packed, and the fans were noisy and enthusiastic. Rockwell called Terrell Sparks as the starting pitcher. Chip took part in a pepper game, chased flies when the Statesmen had batting practice, and then retired to the dugout. His arm felt tired, and he was glad for the rest.

Eastern had a 50-50 conference record, having won three and lost three. Chip had watched the Easterners take their practice batting and didn't think they were too strong with the stick. Fortunately for the Statesmen, they weren't!

Terrell Sparks got into one tight spot after another, but his support was superb, and the visitors were held scoreless for five innings. At the plate, the Statesmen scored six runs, with Biggie contributing a single, a triple, and a home run.

Sparks got into trouble in the top of the sixth. Coach Rockwell called on Doogie Dugan. He sent Green in for Biggie at the same time. Before the inning was over, the visitors scored two runs. With two down and runners on second and third, the hitter slammed a hard grounder to Durley. The third baseman fired a clothesline peg to Green, but the first baseman missed the throw. The ball went clear to the right-field fence, and both runners scored. The batter ended up on third base. The next batter flied out, retiring the side.

The Statesmen came right back with two runs of their own in the bottom of the sixth and scored four more before the game ended. Eastern managed to get another run before it was over. The score: State 13, Eastern 3.

Biggie drove Chip, Soapy, and Fireball to Grayson's after the game and agreed to go with them to Mark Parsons's clinic Sunday afternoon. He was back again that night at 10:30 and drove them home to Jeff.

The next morning, Chip and Soapy were up early and off to church. The pastor's sermon was about the disciples' argument among themselves over who was greatest. It made Chip think about the bickering among his teammates, and he prayed for wisdom in leading both sides of the team.

At 3:30 Sunday afternoon, when the store closed, Biggie drove Chip, Soapy, Speed, and Fireball to the clinic. As soon as he drove up behind the chicken-wire backstop, the car was surrounded. The youngsters were impressed by the players, but they couldn't conceal their admiration for the red car. Mark pushed his way importantly through the gathering, followed by an elderly man whom he introduced as Coach Pop Travis, the team manager. Chip learned that Mr. Travis was a retired truck driver who had taken an interest in the kids in his neighborhood. He enjoyed working with them on their baseball. Chip introduced the man to his friends and asked Coach Travis what he wanted them to do.

"What positions do they all play?" Pop Travis asked, nodding to the other players.

"Smith is a catcher, Biggie plays first base, Speed is a shortstop, Fireball is in center field, and I pitch."

"That covers everything just fine," Travis said happily. "Each one of you can talk about your position and answer any questions the kids want to ask. All right?"

Chip and his friends agreed, and Coach Travis herded the kids to the side of the hill and told them to sit down. It was obvious that Pop Travis was dedicated to kids, and it was clear that the kids respected and appreciated his interest in them. An older group of boys was standing nearby, but they remained where they were, talking in undertones. When the clinic started, Chip forgot all about them.

The clinic was turning into a big success. Mark, his catcher friend, and the rest of the home-run kids were a terrific hit with Chip's pals, and they entered heartily into the spirit of the afternoon's clinic.

Soapy started it off. First, he borrowed the catcher's own glove. He squatted and showed the boys the signs used for various pitches. He enthusiastically illustrated the signs that were flashed to the pitcher and the infielders for pick-off plays and throws from the catcher to the bases. He finished with a discussion of his method of estimating batters' weaknesses. It was *great* stuff, and the kids ate it up.

Biggie followed and did the same thing for the base positions. Speed and Fireball were up next. Chip was last. He showed them how he held the ball for various throws: his power pitch, curve, screwball, and the change-up. Then he discussed pitching form, the windup, concealing the ball from the batter, throwing to the bases, and the pitcher's fielding responsibilities. After he had answered their questions, Chip divided them into groups. Each of his friends took the boys who were interested in their position to a separate spot on the field for demonstrations.

At 5:30 he called them back, and each player discussed batting. A little later Chip called it a day. The kids responded with a cheer. A glance at his pals assured Chip that they had been as charmed by the enthusiasm and appreciation of the kids as he had.

They piled into Abe's car, and Biggie headed for the student union. Chip's heart was filled with a great satisfaction; it had been a great day. The guys shared a couple of pizzas together at their favorite table in the student union and had a lot of fun talking about the youngsters.

When they finished eating, Biggie dropped them off at Jeff and continued on to the hotel to spend the evening with his brother. Chip and the others knew it was time to hit the books and headed to their rooms.

Monday started off as usual. Soapy went through his regular morning routine. He and Chip walked to the union to meet everyone for breakfast. They separated for their classes and met again for lunch. Everyone showed up for lunch with the exception of Fireball and Biggie. Fireball had a class, and Chip figured Biggie was with Abe.

Chip had a short schedule in the afternoon and hustled out to practice so Murph Kelly could work on his arm. After the rubdown, he dressed and went out on the field. He ran twice around the field and finished just as Fireball, Speed, and Red appeared. Rockwell, Malone, and Kelly were right behind them, and the coach waited until the players had finished their laps. Then he blasted his whistle and read off the practice program.

Chip and Dugan were assigned to throw to Engle at the practice pitching rubber near third base. He had just started a throw to Engle when Soapy came out of the players' aisle. Chip held up his throw and handed the ball to Dugan.

Soapy wasn't in his uniform, and Chip immediately knew something was wrong. The redhead spotted him and broke forward at a trot. He was puffing excitedly, and Chip could tell that the redhead was in a high state of agitation.

"What's the matter?" Chip asked.

"Biggie's in trouble!"

CHAPTER 13

Bubble-Gum Batter

"TROUBLE?" Chip echoed Soapy quickly. "What kind of trouble?"

"I don't know. Something about Abe's car."

"Where is Biggie now?"

Soapy shook his head. "I don't know where he is now, but he was in the provost's office just about all day."

"How did you hear about it?"

"In Professor Gill's class. His car was mixed up in it too."

"When did it happen?"

"Last night, I guess," Soapy said uncertainly. "All I heard was that the provost had Biggie and Abe in his office, along with the campus security guys."

"Anyone hurt?"

"I don't think so."

Chip glanced toward Coach Rockwell. "We ought to tell Coach where Biggie is. Get your uniform on, and I'll let him know."

Coach Rockwell listened carefully to Chip's information and then told him to continue his workout. "There isn't anything we can do right now, Chipper," he said. "I'll get on the phone right after practice and see what it's all about."

It was a long practice. Chip could tell that his friends were deeply concerned about Biggie. The five of them—Soapy, Speed, Biggie, Red, and Chip—had been close friends since elementary school. As boys they had spent hours and hours in Chip's backyard. Chip's father had constructed what the kids had come to call the Hilton Athletic Club (A. C.). There were baskets, a goal post, and even a pitcher's mound. After Chip's dad had died, the boys continued to meet at the Hilton A. C., practicing their skills, talking through their problems, and helping one another out. Now, finishing up their junior year at State, they were as close as ever and still pulled together whenever anyone needed help.

Rockwell called an end to the workout and sent the players around the field three times and on to the showers. Soapy, Speed, and Red joined Chip after all had showered. Together they hustled across the campus to Jefferson Hall. Along the way, Chip recalled a Bible verse he learned as a child: "A man who has friends must himself be friendly, but there is a friend who sticks closer than a brother."

Biggie wasn't in his room, and none of the other Jeff residents had seen him all day, so Chip and Soapy headed down to their jobs at Grayson's. Speed said he would wait at the dorm until Biggie showed up. "I'll call you as soon as he gets home," he promised.

Chip had been at work only a few minutes when Speed called and said that Biggie and Abe were on their way down to the store. Fifteen minutes later, Soapy ushered them into the stockroom. Biggie and Abe were both dejected. "Listen to this," Soapy said. "You'll never believe it."

"That's right," Biggie said despondently, dropping down on a chair. "I still can't figure it out. Anyway, I'm on probation *and* the ex-athletics list."

"What!" Chip exclaimed.

Abe nodded. "That's right," he said. "We've been tied up in this thing all day, and we still don't know what actually happened. The school police, or whatever you call them, say Biggie damaged some professor's car and left the scene of the accident."

"Biggie wouldn't do that!" Soapy said indignantly.

"Of course not," Abe said, nodding in agreement.

"I never even had an accident!" Biggie commented. "I tried to tell them I didn't know anything about it, but they wouldn't believe me."

"When did they say all this happened?" Chip asked.

"Last night," Abe said.

Biggie nodded his head to accentuate each word and spoke clearly and slowly, obviously under a strain. "After I let you guys out at the dorm, I went down to the hotel and had dinner with Abe. As you know, I have to be at work in facilities at nine o'clock. I got back about eight o'clock. It was still light. I parked the car and went to work, and I didn't leave the building until this morning. I got up early and decided to drive down to the hotel to see Abe. When I got to the parking lot, the first thing I saw was the busted taillight."

"That's when he made his mistake," Abe interrupted. "He thought someone had backed into my car, and he was afraid I would be angry. So he took the car to a repair shop to have the light fixed."

"As luck would have it," Biggie continued, "right then— while I was still there—the campus police called to find out if anyone had shown up with a busted taillight."

"But how did they know it was Abe's car?" Chip asked.

"They didn't," Biggie answered, "but the glass from Abe's car was scattered on the ground behind this teacher's car. When the mechanic at the garage said he was working on a car with a broken taillight, well, the police came right over. The piece of glass fit."

"Not that Biggie had anything to hide," Abe added quickly.

"It's a mess," Biggie said in disgust.

"Well, *someone* had to be driving Abe's car," Chip mused. "Did you lock the doors?"

"Sure! They were still locked the next morning too."

"How about the keys? You didn't leave them in the car, did you?"

Biggie shook his head vigorously. "No way," he said. "I know I didn't."

"You don't suppose the teacher could have backed into *my* car, do you?" Abe asked with hesitation.

"He would say so if he had," Soapy said emphatically. "He isn't that kind of a man. I know him."

Abe shrugged. "I'm sure you're right. He seemed like a nice enough person. Anyway, he was covered by insurance, and I gave him a check for $150 to take care of the deductible. I don't want you guys to get me wrong; I'm not concerned about my car or the money. I'm worried because Biggie is on probation."

"And," Soapy said gloomily, "ex-athletics."

"He won't be for long," Chip said firmly. "There's an answer to all of this, and I'm going to find it."

"I hope so," Abe said, exhaustion sounding in his voice. "Unfortunately, I've got to leave early tomorrow morning. I don't like to leave when Biggie is in a spot like this, but I have to get back to work. I can't help it."

"Biggie's got us," Chip said quietly.

"Well," Abe said, rising to his feet, "I've got to get going. Get in touch with me if you need me."

Biggie and Abe left then, and Chip spent the rest of the evening trying to figure out the mystery. At closing time, when he and Soapy caught a lift back to the dorm with Fireball in his old yellow VW, Chip had still made no progress. Nothing added up.

He was no closer to the answer on Wednesday when the bus pulled out for Carlton. He thought about it every minute of the two-hour trip but got nowhere. He dressed automatically and was still trying to puzzle it out when he warmed up before the game. When Carlton took the field, he sat down beside Soapy in the dugout and forced thoughts of the situation out of his mind.

Crowell led off for State. The home-team pitcher was wild, and Crowell patiently waited him out, drawing a walk.

Speed bunted down the third-base line, and Crowell lit out for second. The third baseman dashed in, fumbled the ball, saw there was no play at second base, and hurried his throw. The ball went over the first baseman's head as Crowell went on to third, and Speed made it down to second base. Then Fireball blasted a triple, scoring Crowell and Speed.

Green, batting in Biggie's cleanup spot, now walked up to the plate. The cocky first baseman went through all his usual warm-up rituals and then stepped into the batter's box, glaring at the pitcher all the while.

Soapy suddenly exploded into laughter. "Look at that," he cried, elbowing Chip.

Ben Green, with a huge pink bubble extending from his mouth, was staring down the Carlton pitcher. The gigantic bubble and Ben's fierce glare brought a roar from the spectators, and even Chip couldn't resist the urge to laugh. The picture of Ben standing there with a big bubble emerging from his lips could have been taken right out of a comic strip.

The Carlton pitcher fired his fastball down the middle, and Green hit the ball right on the nose. It went high in the air but straight to the left fielder. Fireball tagged up, and when the outfielder caught the ball, he dashed for the plate, beating the throw by twenty feet. Schwartz grounded out. Chip had a three-run cushion behind him when he came to the mound. He set the batters down in order and was in complete control during the rest of the game.

Green's play at first base, compared to Biggie's all-around fielding skill, was terrible. His footwork was faulty, and he was weak on hard-hit ground balls. His arm was strong and fairly accurate, but he lacked Biggie's ability to field a ball swiftly and make a fast peg. He couldn't make the long, graceful stretch so important in meeting the ball and beating a fleet runner at first. At the plate he tried too hard and went zero for four in his turns at bat.

Belter Burke, covering right field in the place of Gillen, banged out another home run to increase his total to seven and tie Biggie for the lead in home runs. Fireball checked in with two circuit blows and raised his total to four. The rest of the bombers hit the ball hard and often, and State University won an easy game, 12-2.

Chip had a chance to talk to Coach Rockwell on the bus trip back to University. He told him everything he had learned about the accident. Rockwell said he had seen Dean Murray and had been told that probation automatically meant an ex-athletic ruling. "It will have to stand until security clears it up," he said gravely.

Later, staring out the window of the darkened bus, Chip reviewed all the points he had discussed with Soapy. *Someone* had driven one of the cars, but how did the person or persons get into the car or cars? Biggie was sure he had locked the doors and taken the keys with him, and perhaps Abe's car hadn't been moved at all. Maybe Professor Gill's car had been moved. And what about the glass? He would see Professor Gill as soon as possible and ask him some questions.

Then Chip began to search for a motive. Had the lights been smashed on purpose? Could it have been the older boys he had seen at the clinic? Would Ben Green have initiated the accident to get Biggie out of the way so he would have a clear shot at first base?

Soapy went along with the assumption that Ben Green was in on it. "That guy would do anything to make the team," Soapy had declared, but Chip didn't believe that sentiment. Despite Green's repulsive behavior, Chip didn't believe Ben measured up to that kind of person. The big player was an extrovert and said what he thought and, Chip felt sure, wouldn't stoop to such an underhanded trick.

The team got back late that night. After checking their E-mails back at the dorm, they hit the sack. Thursday morning Chip went to see Professor Gill. He explained to the young professor that Biggie was a close friend and now on probation.

"I know how you feel, Chip," Gill said kindly. "However, it's out of my hands. As far as I'm concerned, the matter is settled. I told the provost that, but he's a hard man to talk to."

"Do you have any idea how it could have happened?" Chip asked.

"It's beyond me," Gill said, smiling ruefully. "I always lock my car and check the doors. I have never loaned it to anyone. And," he added, "I always park in the same place, in the spot the provost assigned to me, space 20."

Chip had learned absolutely nothing from Professor Gill. He thanked him and went to the student union for lunch. The guys were all there, and they spent an entire hour discussing Biggie's trouble. Shortly before one o'clock, Biggie showed up, despondent and discouraged.

"The chief of campus security says I'm either a clever liar or a sleepwalker," Biggie said, a slight smile playing on his lips. "I've been in his office all morning."

"Are you missing any classes?" Chip asked.

"What difference does it make?" Biggie said bitterly. "I'm through with baseball for the year. Missing classes doesn't mean anything now."

"That's not true," Chip said gently. "I know how much your engineering degree means to you. Chief Madera will clear this thing up in no time."

"Madera!" Biggie snorted. "Huh! Fat chance."

The friends separated for their classes, leaving Biggie staring moodily at his untouched burger and fries.

HOME RUN FEUD

That afternoon Rockwell let the team off with a light batting and fielding drill. Chip, Soapy, and Fireball lit out on the double for Grayson's. Short practices gave them a chance to eat a leisurely dinner before going to work.

After Skip and Lonnie had gone home that night, Chip sat at the desk in the stockroom and listed on a piece of paper the facts he had obtained in the car mystery.

1. Biggie parked Abe's car at 8:00 P.M.
2. Professor Gill's car had been parked all day and evening.
3. Biggie discovered the damaged left tail light on Abe's car on Monday morning at 8:00 A.M.
4. Both cars were locked.
5. One of the pieces of glass found under Professor Gill's car fit the taillight of Abe's car.
6. A smudge of red paint had been found on the left rear fender of Professor Gill's car. The police, according to Biggie, claimed it was from Abe's red car.
7. Apparently there was no motive.

It was time to close up. He tucked the piece of paper carefully in his pocket. Tomorrow, school or no school and game or no game, he was going to see the chief of State's college security, and Mark Parsons.

CHAPTER 14

A Matter of Record

CHIP WAS in the campus security office the next morning at nine o'clock. Five minutes later an officer ushered Chip into Chief Madera's office. The chief was seated behind a large desk with papers spread out before him. He was middle-aged with dark, unruly hair and steady brown eyes, and he was built like a fullback.

Madera reached a long arm across the desk and grasped Chip's hand in a powerful grip. "Glad to meet you, Hilton. You're bigger than you look in a baseball uniform. What can I do for you?"

Chip told him all about Biggie and the years they had been friends and teammates. "Biggie Cohen simply wouldn't lie about anything," he concluded.

"Sometimes people who become involved in automobile accidents become completely different from the people we know in everyday life," Chief Madera said wryly. "They blow their stacks, clam up, exaggerate, lie, or even pretend to have a loss of memory. I know about Benjamin Cohen, of course. I've seen him play football and baseball, and I know his school record is good. However, nothing can be done about his probation until the investigation is complete and the incident is written off the books. Unfortunately, his failure to report the accident is a matter of record."

"Is there a charge against him?"

"Not a charge, Hilton, but it is recorded on the security blotter, and the case is still open. There's no way to get the case off the blotter until the matter is cleared up."

"But Professor Gill—"

Madera interrupted him. "I know," he said, nodding his head understandingly. "I know all about that. The amount of damage is not important. The big issue is that Professor Gill reported the accident and Benjamin Cohen did not. It's that simple.

"I'm sure you've read in the campus papers that we've been experiencing considerable trouble with student cars: speeding on campus, reckless driving, and illegal parking. It's common knowledge. Because of the incidents that have occurred, the administration has taken a firm stand on the enforcement of rules and regulations. The fact that Cohen didn't know he was supposed to report the matter has nothing to do with it. Ignorance of a regulation is not acceptable."

"Couldn't the provost remove him from the ex-athletics list?"

Madera smiled and answered Chip with his own question. "And break one of his own regulations?"

Chip's hopes fell. "What's the next move?" he asked. "We sure do need Biggie."

"I know," Madera said kindly. "By the way, would you like to ride down to the parking lot with me?"

"I sure would."

"Come along then," Madera replied, putting on his officer's hat and grabbing a set of keys off a rack behind his desk.

The chief drove to the parking lot, and they got out of the car. Chip followed Madera as he showed him where the cars had been parked. "Cohen parked his brother's car directly opposite space 20," Madera explained. "The numbered spaces are reserved, and we assign them to department heads and professors. The spaces on the opposite side are open to visitors on a first come-first serve basis."

There wasn't much to see. Just below the parking lot on the right was the ballfield where he and the guys had given the clinic to the home-run kids on Sunday. Beyond that, there were a small wooded area and, rising against the horizon a few blocks away, the towers of the engineering and medical colleges.

"There's not much to go on," Madera said ruefully. "There are no witnesses that we can find and no evidence except the busted taillights and a few pieces of glass."

Chief Madera drove Chip back to the campus and dropped him off in front of the main entrance to the student union. He took down Chip's phone numbers at the dormitory and at Grayson's and promised to call if any new developments occurred.

Chip went to his eleven o'clock class and then joined his friends for lunch. Game time was three o'clock, so he limited his food to fruit salad and a light sandwich. Afterward, he went into the student union lounge and, sitting at a desk by the window, drew a sketch of the parking lot and the positions of the two involved cars. Then he walked to Alumni Field, dressed, and went out on the diamond.

As Rockwell had said, it was an important series. A double win for the Statesmen could knock Midwestern out of the conference race and strengthen State's position at the top of the league.

Rockwell started Dean. The tall lefty was wild, but his support was sensational. Midwestern had men on base every inning but couldn't get them around. The visiting hurler was good, pitched heady baseball, and kept ahead of the hitters. The result was a scoreless tie at the end of six innings.

Chip was absorbed in the game, but he noticed with satisfaction that the home-run kids were roaming the fences. He breathed a sigh of relief when he located Mark Parsons among them. If Mark would only stick around after the game, he could talk to him.

With one down in the top of the sixth, Dean worked himself into a jam. He walked the first batter and then made the mistake of feeding the middle cleanup hitter a fastball on the outside. The batter connected, and the ball sailed over the left-field fence to put Midwestern in the lead 2-0.

Dean served up another walk, and the next batter beat out a bunt. With men on first and second, the batter drove a hard grounder over third base. Durley made a backhand stop and pegged the ball to Crowell to get the first runner. Crowell then made the relay to Ben Green to complete the double play. Burke pulled in a long fly for out number three and the Statesmen headed in. They managed to squeeze in a run in the bottom frame to make the score Midwestern 2, State 1 at the end of six full innings.

The teams battled evenly through the seventh and eighth innings with neither club able to score. Then, in the top of the ninth, Dean had one of his wild spells and walked the first two batters. Rockwell called time and held a conference with Engle and the lefty. It called for a tough decision. Sparks and Dugan had been warming up for the past three innings. Rockwell debated the matter for a time and then called for Dugan.

Doogie took his eight warm-up pitches and got the first batter when he fielded a bunt and threw the batter out at first. It was one away with runners on second and third.

The next Midwestern batter also bunted. The ball spun in front of the plate, and Engle fielded it perfectly. He faked a throw to third base to hold the lead runner and then fired the ball to Green. The throw had the batter by a mile, but the third-base runner dashed for home, and Green, trying to throw the ball before he caught it, fumbled. Before he could recover the ball, the lead runner scored and the man on second went to third.

The batter was safe at first.

The next batter hit a hard grounder deep in the shortstop hole. Speed cut to his right and made an almost impossible stop. His throw to Crowell got the man coming into second base, and the little second baseman's relay to Green completed the double play to retire the side. The Statesmen came in for their last licks with the score Midwestern 3, State 1.

Crowell led off, waited for a good one, and beat out a drag bunt. Fireball strolled out to the on-deck circle as Speed advanced to the plate. Assistant Coach Bill Malone flashed the sign for the hit-and-run, and Speed stepped into the batter's box. The Midwestern pitcher was being careful now. Too careful! He tried to get Speed on two bad throws in a row, but Speed was waiting for a good one.

Crowell took a big lead as the pitcher came in with a slow curve. It was headed for the strike zone, waist-high. It almost seemed that Speed waited too long to swing, but just as the second baseman dashed for the keystone sack, Speed punched a sharp hit to the right of second base and through the hole. Crowell turned second like a scared rabbit and lit out for third base. The center fielder came in fast and fielded the ball cleanly, but Crowell made third base standing up. Speed held up at first. It was a perfect execution of Andre Durley's "inside" baseball! The tying run was on base!

Fireball was up. The fans were going wild. As he started toward the plate, the Midwestern coach called time. After a short consultation with the battery, he went back to the visiting team's dugout, shaking his head worriedly. The Midwestern pitcher threw three straight fastballs, and Fireball managed to tip each one of them. The catcher held on to the third foul for the first out. That setback deflated the crowd only momentarily.

Ben Green strode to the plate with the stage all set for him to be the hero. The fans were tearing down the stands, imploring Green to pulverize the ball, to knock it over the fence and out of the park. They cheered for him to blast a home run, bring the ducks in, and win the game! All his animosity forgotten, Chip joined in the tumult, yelling for Green as loudly and as enthusiastically as the rest of the Statesmen.

Ben went through his prebatting ritual before he stepped up to the plate. No one in the stadium could hear himself think, the excitement was so great. The pitcher powered in his heater, a fast one close to the wrists. Green started his swing, saw that the pitch was too close, and tried to hold up. But he couldn't stop, and his bat hit the ball, sending it high in the air and back toward the grandstand. To the despair of every State fan in the park, the Midwestern catcher easily gloved the ball and trotted back to the plate.

Two away! State runners still perched on the corners. The crowd grew silent. The score: Midwestern 3, State 1.

Schwartz had been in the on-deck circle swinging the warm-up bat. Before he could move toward the plate, however, Rockwell called time and grabbed Chip by the arm. "Get in there for Schwartz," he said breathlessly. "Take your time! The steal is on, and if you bat lefty and stay close to the plate, it will be tougher for the catcher to make the throw to second. Got it?"

"I sure do, Coach," Chip said, nodding.

"They *may* try a cutoff play. Crowell will be faking to come home to draw the throw. If Speed makes it down to second, you're on your own. Look the first pitch over anyway."

Chip got his bat from the rack, and Bobby Traymore ran out with the substitution slip. The plate umpire announced, "Hilton now batting for Schwartz," as Chip walked out to the plate. Red handed him the warm-up bat and held Chip's bat while he took a couple of practice swings. Chip focused on what he needed to do and blocked out everything but the directions the Rock had given him. This was the kind of baseball Chip liked—Andre Durley's kind, the kind that put the team first.

"Slow and easy, Chipper," Red said fervently, slapping him on the back.

Chip took his bat and walked around to the lefty batter's box. Stepping into the box, he pulled the bat through a couple of times and concentrated on the pitcher. The Midwestern hurler threw a fastball to the right of the plate, shoulder-high. Speed was well on his way to second as the catcher threw the ball.

The shortstop covered the bag, but the second baseman cut off the throw and fired the ball home. Crowell had faked beautifully, but now he retreated to third. Speed was perched safely on second base.

The pitcher was wary now. He threw to the corners and pitched himself into a hole. With the count at three and zero, he was forced to come in with a good pitch. Chip tagged it. The ball sailed over first base and landed a yard inside the white foul line.

Tearing around first base, he saw the right fielder come up with the ball and peg it in to the plate. Chip kept going but saw Crowell cross the plate with Speed right behind him. The two-bagger had tied the score at 3-3.

Belter Burke was up next, and it was obvious that the powerful hitter wasn't going for anything except a pitch in the strike zone. The pitcher tried a curve around the letters. Belter leaned into the ball.

C-r-a-c-k!

On his way to third, Chip turned his head just in time to see the ball sail over the right-field fence. He continued on in to home plate and joined the entire State team in waiting to greet Burke.

Belter slowly circled the bases and jogged home. His ecstatic teammates hoisted him to their shoulders. They had won 5-3! The Statesmen had kept their undefeated record intact, had won nine games in a row, and were in undisputed possession of first place in the conference.

Chip showered and dressed quickly, hoping to catch the home-run kids, but he could have taken an hour. Mark Parsons and all the home-run kids were waiting to add their praises to those of the fans. Mark met Chip and held out a card. Chip signed it, thinking it was probably the tenth wrinkled Nolan Ryan, Roger Clemens, or Orel Hershiser card he had autographed.

Chip handed the card back to Mark and asked, "May I have your phone number?"

Mark nodded.

Chip borrowed another one of Mark's cards and wrote the boy's number on the back. "Will you be home at seven?"

Mark studied Chip's face for a moment. "Sure," he said.

"Don't tell anyone I'm going to call."

"I won't," the boy said. He hesitated a moment and then spoke again. "I know what you want to ask me."

Before Chip could say a word, Mark turned swiftly and joined his companions.

Soapy and Fireball came along a few seconds later. The three of them made their way slowly through the crowd of fans and headed quickly for Grayson's. On the way they discussed the highlights of the game, enjoying the exhilarating thrill of victory.

The news of the win had preceded them, and the store was crowded with customers. Many of them congratulated the three on the team's success. Chip worked until seven and then went to one of the booths in the store. He dialed Mark Parsons's phone number, eager to talk to the boy.

He heard the receiver click as it was lifted from the cradle and a woman's voice answered. Before Chip could speak, the woman said, "You must be Chip Hilton. Mark has been sitting here beside the phone for the past hour."

"Yes, ma'am. I hope it isn't a problem that I'm calling at this time."

"No problem at all. Let me just get Mark for you."

Chip talked briefly to Mark, and the boy promised to meet him at the parking lot the next morning.

CHAPTER 15

Apart at the Seams

MARK PARSONS studied the drawing and shook his head in amazement. "Everything's just right," he said, glancing up at Chip in admiration.

"Sure!" Soapy agreed dryly. "Everything's right except the broken taillights and the mystery of who is the responsible person."

"It's a mystery all right," Mark concluded.

"Professor Gill's car was in space 20," Chip explained.

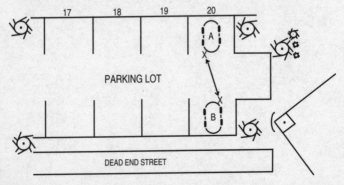

"The letter A represents his car. Biggie's car was parked in the space on this side of the paper, see? The letter B represents his car. One of the cars backed into the other, but neither of the owners knows anything about it. Both cars were locked, so it had to be someone else. I've got to find out who that someone else was."

"Maybe it was a *bunch* of someones," Soapy observed.

"You see, Mark," Chip said quietly, looking into the young boy's face, "Biggie Cohen can't play baseball until we prove he didn't do it."

"Biggie Cohen plays first base, doesn't he?" Mark asked seriously.

"That's right."

"Ben Green will take his place, won't he?"

"That'll be the day," Soapy growled.

"Most of the kids say Ben is the best player," Mark said, looking at Soapy.

Soapy laughed. "Someone has been feeding you a lot of baloney," he said. "Ben Green can't carry Biggie's spikes."

"Biggie is really great, Mark, one of the best first basemen in the country and a great hitter," Chip said earnestly. "I sure wish you could help us."

"Well, I heard some of the guys talking about it," Mark said uncertainly, "but I don't know anything for sure."

"It had to happen at night," Chip said tentatively.

"I'm not allowed over here after supper," Mark said apologetically. "You see, I don't do very well in school and I have to study."

"Do you know anyone who might help me?"

Mark shook his head vigorously. "No, I don't." He debated something for a moment and then reached in his pocket and pulled out a handful of bubble gum cards. "Can I have back the Nolan Ryan card? The one you wrote my telephone number on?" he asked, eyeing Chip closely.

"Sure, Mark."

"I'll give you another one. I'm a pitcher, and I only save pictures of pitchers. I've got a lot of flip cards though."

"Flip cards?"

Mark nodded. "Trading cards—the ones I don't collect."

"You don't save pictures of players who play other positions?"

"Nope. None of us do that. We only save pictures of big-leaguers who play *our* positions."

Chip pulled the Nolan Ryan bubble gum card out of his pocket. "I'll copy your phone number on the new card," he said.

Mark shuffled quickly through the pack of cards. Chip noticed he had pictures of catchers, infielders, outfielders, and a few managers, but he seemed to be looking intently for a particular card. When he had gone through the pack he shook his head in annoyance and went through them once more, checking each card carefully.

"Any card will do," Chip said.

"No, it won't," Mark said stubbornly. "I was saving one for you." He kept looking at the cards and finally came to the one he wanted. "Here it is!" he said broadly, smiling as he handed it to Chip.

The picture showed a first baseman making a one-hand catch. Chip glanced at it and then turned it over and copied Mark's number from the other card.

"Why that card?" Soapy asked.

"I don't like first basemen," Mark said crossly.

"Well, thanks, Mark," Chip said earnestly. "We've got to go. If you find out anything, let me know."

"I will," Mark said, "but remember, I never told you anything."

"I know," Chip said. "Thanks anyway."

"And Chip, be sure you don't lose that card," Mark said, turning away.

Chip and Soapy went to Grayson's and worked until noon. After a sandwich at the fountain, they lit out for

Alumni Field. They were the first players to arrive in the locker room. Murph Kelly gave Chip's arm a long, gentle rubdown.

"You've been pitching too hard and too often," Kelly growled. "It isn't good for a young player like you to go all out every three or four days. Let's see, we played the first game on April seventeen and this is the ninth of May. That's only twenty-two days. If you work this afternoon, it will be six games you've pitched in twenty-two days. That's too much! Mark my words, you're going to end up with a bum arm."

"My arm is fine, Murph," Chip said quickly. "Sure, it gets a little tired during a game, but the next day it's all right."

"Someday it's gonna *stay* tired," Kelly retorted.

Chip knew better than to argue with Murph Kelly. He would only lose. He winked at Soapy and put on his uniform as fast as he could. Soapy was waiting when he finished, and they quickly headed out to the field. Midwestern was holding batting practice, and Chip watched its hitters while he warmed up.

His teammates arrived one by one, and when it was time for them to hold their hitting practice, all members were present except Biggie. Chip glanced at the stands and was amazed. The fans seemed to have come all at once. Every seat was filled, and he could tell by the cheers and yells that the fans were keyed up for another thriller.

Coach Rockwell started him on the rubber with Soapy behind the plate. Green, Crowell, Durley, and Speed made up the infield and Schwartz, Finley, and Burke were in the outfield.

The chatter was there, and he felt good, but Biggie's absence affected him strangely. He felt as if he were playing with only half a team behind him. He didn't let it affect his pitching though. He struck out the first hitter, forced the push-along batter to hit a grounder to Crowell for an easy out at first, and struck out the third Midwesterner on three straight pitches.

Crowell led off when the Statesmen came to bat and promptly lined a single to left field. Speed Morris and Ozzie Crowell combined on one of their inside baseball specialties, the hit-and-run. Crowell started his steal, and when the shortstop moved to cover the bag, Speed punched the ball through the hole for a clean single. That put Crowell on second with Speed on first base. Fireball Finley banged out a triple to score them both. Ben Green tried to knock the cover off the ball and struck out.

Red Schwartz grounded out, the ball going from the pitcher to first. Belter Burke drove a high fly over second base, and the ball carried all the way to the center-field fence. Running at top speed, the fielder made an over-the-shoulder catch that drew cheers from the fans. Fireball died on third base.

It wasn't much of a game. Chip had good support and was never in trouble. Burke and Soapy each hit home runs, and Fireball registered two. When the Statesmen took the field at the top of the ninth, they were leading 7-0.

The first batter in the ninth to face Chip flied to right field. Burke pulled the ball in easily. Chip struck out the next hitter, one-two-three. The third batter hit a foul behind the plate that Soapy caught and proudly tucked in his pocket.

The game was over; the Statesmen didn't even need their last time at bat! They walked off the field with an undefeated string of ten straight victories.

The locker room was the scene of celebration. The Statesmen were riding cloud nine. At the height of the jubilation Coach Rockwell made one of his unusual after-game appearances in the locker room. Murph Kelly immediately yelled for order.

The coach began soberly enough. "Congratulations. It was a nice win and good, solid baseball too. As a little reward for the tough schedule we've faced, curfew rules are off for the weekend. There will be no practice until Wednesday. Remember our next five games are on the road, beginning with Southwestern.

"SWU has a record of ten and one. They are in second place and will be ready for us. Have a good time and get some rest, but remember, the season is far from over. We have eleven big games to go."

The team, excited about the time off, cheered the coach until he walked out the door. Chip was especially thankful for the breather. He would now have an entire week to rest his arm and concentrate on Biggie's problem. By Saturday, Chip hoped, the Statesmen would have their regular first baseman back.

Soapy hadn't said a word since he came back with the papers. With elbows resting on his desk, his head propped between his hands, he was staring moodily out the window. The Sunday *Herald* and *News* were lying untouched on the edge of the redhead's still unmade bed. Chip felt the same way about the newspapers. He didn't care if he never read another sports page as long as he lived.

It didn't seem possible that the fortunes of a team or a person could change so disastrously so quickly. *In just two weeks, fourteen little days,* he reflected.

Chip thought back to the team's locker room celebration right after the Midwestern victory. Then, the Statesmen were leading the league, riding high, sailing along on an undefeated streak of ten games. He had been the best pitcher in State's history, or so Jim Locke had said in the *News*. In his column in the *Herald,* Bill Bell had tabbed Chip Hilton the greatest college pitcher he had seen in forty years of baseball writing.

Two weeks later, at this very moment, State was in third place in the conference race with a record of *ten* wins and *four* losses. The Statesmen were far behind Southwestern and Northern, who were tied for the lead with identical records of fourteen and two.

And, Chip reflected bitterly, he couldn't even last a whole game. He had been charged with three losses in a row and couldn't throw his fastball to the plate if his life depended on it.

It still almost seemed as if it hadn't happened. *It couldn't have happened!* Maybe it was all a bad dream, or perhaps "nightmare" was the right word.

He thought back to the first of the five away games, the Southwestern game. He had started off just as he had against the Midwesterners pitching shutout ball until the ninth inning. Ahead 3-0, the Statesmen were just three outs away from their eleventh straight win.

Then—and he had gone over this a thousand times—it had happened!

He could see it in his mind's eye even now, it was exactly as it had actually happened in the game. Every detail was crystal clear. The first hitter in the top of the ninth had hit a sharp grounder to Durley.

Andre had played the ball just right. He had fielded it on the bounce and fired a blazing peg to first base. The throw had been a little high, but it should have been an easy catch. Ben Green had tried a one-hand show-off catch, flinging his glove hand nonchalantly up in the air. Because of his carelessness, the ball had gotten away from him.

The hitter had sped on to second base. The next batter hit a roller right at Green. It had been hit hard, but the ball should have been easy to handle. Ben Green didn't get down far enough or fast enough, however, and the ball had gone through his legs and on out to right field. Burke, backing up the play, came in fast and fielded the ball.

The lead runner had played it safe until the ball went through Green's legs. Then he darted toward third. Burke made the throw to Durley, but the runner beat the ball and slid safely into the base. The runner on first went to second.

Chip shuddered as he thought of the next play.

The State infield had moved up, looking for the bunt. Sure enough, the batter had bunted down the first-base line. Soapy had blocked the plate and was all set for the throw, but Green was slow in fielding the ball. Trying to make up for the delay, he fired it way over Soapy's head. Two runners made it home before Soapy recovered the ball, and two more Southwestern runners were perched on second and third. There was no one down.

With the tying run on third base and the winning run on second, Chip had pitched as he had never pitched before. He had struck out the next two hitters. The count on the third batter, a righty, had gone to two and two.

Then, Chip Hilton had made the pitch he would never forget.

Soapy had called for the slider, and Chip had put every bit of his power into the throw. The ball shot in toward the plate shoulder-high. Then it seemed to rise. It sailed straight at the batter's head. The batter tried to get out of the way, but the ball had cracked into his jaw with a sickening thud. The batter toppled to the ground like a falling tree.

The plate umpire called time, but no one heard him. The Southwestern players and fans charged him. A fist-throwing melee raged. The umpires, Rockwell, Malone, and the Southwestern coach quickly broke it up and cleared the field, but the Southwestern players and fans continued to boo and shout at him.

Chip had felt sick. He *still* felt sick! The ambulance had arrived, and the medical team had carried the unconscious player from the field. Rockwell had talked to Chip in the dugout during the interim and urged him to stay in the game, to finish it out. Chip had wanted to make way for Dean or Sparks, but Rockwell was adamant.

"It's the right thing to do, Chip. You can't whip anything by running away from it."

He knew then as he knew now that the Rock had been right.

When the game resumed, the Southwestern coach sent up a pinch hitter, a lefty. The fans kept up a steady stream of boos, adding further to Chip's perturbation. It was the first time he had ever been subjected to such abuse and animosity. His control was completely disrupted.

Soapy called for a fastball, but Chip shook him off. He wanted to throw it but was caught, bound by a mental block he couldn't break. He tried, but it was as if he were paralyzed. He couldn't force himself to throw it. Soapy had no recourse except to call for curves and change-up pitches. The count went to three and two.

Then, in sheer desperation and with nothing on the ball but hope, Chip tried his knuckler. With two away, the runners were on the move. The lefty went for the pitch and hit it with the handle of his bat.

The result was a little looping fly ball coming in directly over Green's head. Chip had breathed a sigh of relief and taken off his glove. Holding it in his right hand, he was poised to head for the dugout as soon as Green caught the ball.

Green waited, his eyes concentrating on the ball. He raised his glove and free hand to make the catch, but then he dropped the ball!

Two runs were scored before the fumbling Green recovered it. The next batter flied out to Finley. The Statesmen came in to bat trailing Southwestern by one, 3-4, and the game ended that way. The SWU pitcher set the State hitters down in one-two-three order, and the Statesmen lost their first game of the season right then.

But that was just the beginning!

Coach Rockwell had started him against Midwestern on the following Wednesday. It was the second game of the away series. Chip wanted to prove to himself he had forgotten the SWU incident, but as soon as he faced the first batter, he broke out in a cold sweat.

This time Soapy didn't even call for a fastball. Without his dazzling speed and the screwball or slider, Chip Hilton was just another pitcher. The Midwesterners knocked him out of the box in the second inning. They were hitting hard and kept it up, running Dean and Sparks to the showers too. They gave little Doogie Dugan a terrific shellacking before the game ended. The State hitters hadn't gotten over the shock of the Southwestern defeat and couldn't put together what few hits they got. Midwestern coasted to an easy win, 12-2.

Cathedral had capped off the week by taking both games of the weekend series, winning by identical scores Friday and Saturday, 6-1. He hadn't even lasted out the first inning in the Saturday game.

The Statesmen hadn't taken their losses very gracefully either.

Chip had come in for some veiled criticism, but Green had been the real target. The regulars were bitter and antagonistic and placed the blame for the week's debacle squarely on the cocky first baseman's shoulders. They wouldn't let him forget his mistakes and mercilessly got on Ben Green's back and stayed there.

To Chip's surprise, Gillen, Engle, Nickels, and Dean joined in with the others and took their turns at recalling the passed ball, the fumbled bunt, the overthrow, and the dropped fly.

The Statesmen had completely and disastrously come apart at the seams. Ben Green fought back at first. He snarled and blustered and tried to shrug it off, but he couldn't fight them all and he couldn't win, and he finally lapsed into a sullen silence.

Green's collapse had brought thoughts of Biggie. Chip hadn't forgotten the car trouble, but his own downfall had been so complete and devastating that he had been unable to think clearly about his pal's problem.

Chip knew they couldn't sit there all day and keep this attitude going. He glanced at Soapy. The redhead's spirit was broken. All the old pep and vivacity that were so much a part of Soapy's personality were gone.

"Come on, we need to go to church," Chip said in a low voice, pulling on his shoes. "It's been a black week."

The two friends headed for church, walking slowly and each buried in his own thoughts. Chip always appreciated going to church because it helped him to reflect on the past week and to gain focus for what was coming in the next week. The people of the University church were friendly and greeted them warmly, always happy to see them.

Chip pushed down the feelings he was carrying and concentrated on listening to what the pastor was saying. Most Sundays he listened attentively and took notes, but today he couldn't seem to focus on what the pastor was saying. *What are we going to do?* he wondered.

CHAPTER 16

And All the Dreams

MONDAYS COULD BE bluer than blue, and as bad as things were, they got worse. Chip found this out first thing the next morning. When he arrived for his nine o'clock class, a note on the door stated the professor was ill and the class had been canceled. Chip decided to use the time to do a little extra work in the science lab. He had just gotten settled at one of the lab tables when a classmate sat down beside him.

"More trouble, right, Hilton?" the classmate said.

"More?" Chip echoed. "What do you mean?"

"Absences. Didn't you hear? Burke, Cohen, and Finley all had too many absences."

"It can't be," Chip said in disbelief.

"Sorry, but their names are posted on the board outside Dean Murray's office."

"Are you sure?"

"Positive! Does that mean they can't play anymore this year?"

"I guess so," Chip said slowly, trying to collect his thoughts. He felt as if all the strength had been drained from his body. He snapped shut the lab book he had opened and laced the fingers of his hands firmly together. Despite the past black week, he hadn't given up; he had felt sure everything would turn out all right. But this was almost too much.

That does it! he told himself. *There goes the championship and all the dreams.*

"How many games do you guys have left?" the other boy asked.

"Seven," Chip said numbly.

"What happened to you guys last week?"

Chip's temper flared. What did this guy think happened? Didn't he read the papers? Why all the questions? Chip took a deep breath and forced back the angry words that were on the tip of his tongue. He had asked himself that question all weekend, and he might as well get used to others asking it.

"It was my fault," he managed. "I went to pieces after the SWU player was beaned."

The other student looked at him and smiled with sympathy. "You weren't the only one," he said kindly. "The whole team went to pieces." The boy's face reflected a mixture of disappointment and sympathy. "I feel sorry for you," he added.

Chip glanced appreciatively at him and turned away. He opened his lab book again and leafed through the pages. Then it hit him like a slap across the face. Without thinking, he had absorbed this guy's pity like a big, soft sponge! It was a slap at his pride, his courage, and his leadership!

Suddenly the blood rushed to his face and he was flooded with a sense of shame. *Sorry!* The fellow was actually sorry for him, and he had sopped it up like a spineless fish.

He wanted to crawl into a hole until he could rid himself of the sense of shame. Obeying a sudden impulse, he gathered up his books and, head down, walked out of the room. He didn't know where he was going, but he had to find a place where he could do some quiet thinking.

Several fellow students spoke to him, but he merely nodded and kept going until he was out of the building and on the campus walkway.

He had no destination in mind. He simply hurried along, feeling like a scared rabbit looking for a place to hide. He came to the library and walked up the broad steps, through the lobby, and into one of the small reading rooms. Chip continued on to the far corner and sat down at a small study table. There he opened a book and stared at the page without seeing a single word on the printed page. *Lord,* he prayed, *help me!*

Chip's thoughts rambled a lot during the rest of the morning but always came back to the same conclusion—his personal failure as the team captain to keep fighting. The fact that he had beaned a player was nothing to be ashamed of; he hadn't tried to. He'd never tried to bean anyone in his life. He had let guilt go too far, and now he needed to stop. He had made a mistake; it was that simple.

Yes, he mused, if the team was demoralized and had come apart at the seams, it was *his* fault. He could sit there all day looking for an alibi, but he wouldn't find one. He had let his pitching get him down and forgotten that he was supposed to hold the team together and keep fighting, no matter what the odds.

Well, he reflected, maybe it wasn't too late to start. And the time to start was right now! He decided to jot down exactly what should be done, in order. He fished in his backpack for a pencil. His hand touched the card Mark Parsons had given him. He pulled the card out and placed it face-up on the opened book. Glancing at it, he saw the picture of the first baseman, and under the picture, the name of the player.

It didn't register at first. Then, suddenly, the pieces began to fall together. His heart leaped in excitement. The Statesmen and Chip Hilton had hit bottom, but maybe this was the turning point!

Just as he looked at his watch, Chip heard the first of twelve gongs from the student union bell tower. He couldn't believe his eyes or ears. Twelve o'clock! Where had the morning gone? He was straining at the wire now and could scarcely wait until he would see Soapy. He almost ran across the daffodil-studded lawns to the student union. As soon as he entered the cafeteria, he saw Soapy, Speed, Fireball, and Red seated at the group's regular table. Walking over to join them, he stilled his excitement and sat down calmly. A quick glance at their plates showed him that all four of his pals had selected light lunches. None of them were making much of a pretense of enjoying the food.

"I suppose you've heard the bad news," Red said tentatively.

"You mean the class absences?" He turned to Fireball. "Fireball, how could you let it happen?"

The center fielder eyed him for a moment and then looked down at his bowl of soup. "I'm sorry, Chip. I lost count and skipped a couple of classes last week just before the trip."

"You didn't check with the dean's office? What about Burke?"

Fireball shrugged and shook his head ruefully. "I was sure I had cuts left. Burke forgot to count the four baseball trips."

"Now we *are* up against it," Soapy said forlornly.

"Especially when we're four back in the win column and have two more losses than SWU and Northern," Speed said. "Man, there's no way we can make all that up in seven games."

"You don't know until you try," Chip said quickly. "Besides, you're overlooking something. We play SWU twice at home. We finish the season with Northern, and *that's* at home. All we have to do is win the rest of our games."

"All? That's all we have to do?" Red echoed bitterly. "We haven't got a chance, Chip! We won't have any of our big hitters and—" he hesitated for a moment—"well, we're hurting for pitching."

"We've *been* hurting," Chip said grimly. "That's all over."

"We need to do something about the team," Soapy said worriedly. "We can't quit."

"From the way you all talk and act," Chip said, "it looks like we already have."

"We haven't quit, Chip," Speed said softly. "If you're all right, we're all right."

"We've still got a good team," Chip said resolutely. "It just means we have to fight harder."

"We'll fight!" Red gritted, banging his fist on the table to show his support.

"Good! We've got to get the rest of the team feeling that way too. We've all got to get up on our hind legs and fight like crazy. Especially me!"

"You think you'll be all right?" Fireball asked solicitously.

"I've *got* to be!"

"You've had a lot on your mind, that's for sure," Red said.

"That's all over," Chip said confidently. "Right now, there's a lot to be done."

"Biggie?" Speed said suggestively.

"Right."

"That's going to take time," Soapy said.

"Maybe not. Do you have a class?"

"Nope."

"Good! Come on. We've got to figure something out. See you fellows at practice."

"You won't see me," Fireball said ruefully. "Not until next year anyway."

It was an awkward moment. Chip shook his head and turned slowly away, searching for something to say. It wouldn't help matters to blurt out the words that came so readily to mind.

It had been Fireball's own fault, he thought unhappily, and Burke's too. Biggie had *some* excuse but not enough.

None of them were grade school kids. Studies came first, and there wasn't any excuse for missing classes.

He led the way out of the cafeteria, and they all headed in different directions. He and Soapy settled in at a table in the corner of the lounge. Soapy was bursting with curiosity. As soon as they were situated, the redhead placed his elbows on the table and leaned forward. "What gives? What's up?" he asked.

"A red car. Do you remember our conversation with Mark Parsons that day at the campus parking lot?"

"Sure, most of it."

"You remember that he said he and the other kids saved only pictures of the big-league players who played their positions?"

"Yes."

"Well, look at this card. Does it mean anything to you?"

"Not particularly. Oh! Wait—Moose Skowron!"

"That's right. A first baseman," Chip said pointedly. "Bill 'Moose' Skowron."

Soapy's eyes widened. "Now I get it!" he said excitedly, "Moose Green! Sure! That's it! In the stockroom Skip said Ben Green's nickname was Moose."

"Right. Do you remember Mark saying, 'Remember, I didn't *tell* you anything' or something like that? Didn't that strike you as peculiar at the time?"

"Sure! Sure it did."

"And he said something about my being sure not to lose the card."

Soapy nodded vigorously. "You've got something, Chip. Ben Green plays first base, and his nickname is Moose. I knew it! I knew that guy was in on it. He planned the whole thing and—"

"No, no," Chip interrupted, shaking his head. "You're wrong. Mark wasn't trying to tell us about Ben; he was trying to tell us about Marty Green. Remember when he said Marty ran around with a bunch of toughs and older boys?"

"Yes, but—"

"And right after I said it happened at night, Mark took particular pains to say that *he* didn't play there at night but that *Marty* did. Remember?"

Soapy scratched his head doubtfully. "You really think Mark is that smart?" he asked.

"I've got to."

"All right," Soapy said resolutely, "let's go! We'll ask him straight up."

"No, that won't solve it. I've got to put it up to Ben."

"*Ben!*" Soapy repeated. "You mean you're going to tell Ben that Marty was in on the car trouble?"

"I sure am!"

"You're going to end up in a fight."

"That's a chance I'll have to take. Besides, I've been thinking about a showdown with Ben Green for a long, long time. This is as good a time as any."

"He's fifty pounds heavier than you are!"

"It makes no difference. Anyway, it's just the start. There are a couple of other guys on the team I intend to straighten out. Today!"

Soapy stared at Chip in surprise. "You really meant it about getting up on your hind legs and fighting, didn't you?"

"I sure did! I wonder when Green gets out of class?"

"I don't know, but he always comes to practice from the direction of the gym."

"I hope he comes that way today."

"I'm going with you."

"Not a chance," Chip said firmly. "Then there would *really* be a fight."

"You're making a mistake."

"I'll soon find out," Chip said lightly. "See you at practice, Soapy."

He left Soapy sitting at the table shaking his head with misgivings. On the way to the gym, Chip was suddenly beset with similar feelings. Perhaps he was moving too fast and giving Mark too much credit for shrewdness. Perhaps he was reading things into Mark's words that the little guy didn't mean. Then Chip recalled what Mark had said when he asked the boy about his telephone number: *I know what you want to ask me.*

Chip waited on the sidewalk by the gym. He soon recognized the swaggering walk of Ben Green, on his way to practice. Stepping directly into his path, Chip began immediately.

"We need to talk, Ben."

Green, chewing hard on his bubble gum, looked wary. "Something wrong, captain?"

"I think you know exactly what's wrong. Your attitude has been ripping this team apart."

"What attitude?" Green muttered.

"The attitude you're showing me right now. The one that says you're better than everybody else. The one that makes you act like you've got to be some sort of baseball superman to be a part of the team. The one that makes you want to murder the ball. And—" Chip hesitated—"the one that makes you go after balls you know you can never get."

"I don't think I'm better than anyone else!" the big first baseman snarled. "I'm just trying to do my best."

"I know that, Ben. And believe it or not, I've been rooting for you all along."

"Huh?" Green looked up, surprise in his eyes.

"Maybe you haven't noticed, but I believe in the *team*. Not just Soapy, Speed, Biggie, and the rest of the guys I've played with for years, but all of the team. Every member. I *want* you to succeed. I want you to knock the cover off the ball, Ben. You're one of the biggest hitters I've ever seen— better than me, if you want to know the truth."

"What are you driving at?" Green asked suspiciously.

"That all your grandstanding has hurt us. It's ripped the team apart. This game isn't about hitting home runs; it's about winning. That means pitching, fielding, running the bases . . . and, yes, scoring some runs. I'm sorry if I've made it sound like I'm against the long ball, Ben, because I'm not. But more than hitting a bunch of balls over the fence, I want our team to win."

"Well . . ." Ben Green hesitated. "Me too."

"Then it's time to help me make this a *team*. Don't make speeches about hitters being better than pitchers. And don't feel you've got to grab every ball that's hit. We're all in this together, Ben."

"I'm doing the best I can!"

"I know that. And we're all going to support you. You're our starting first baseman for the rest of the season—Biggie won't be allowed back on the team. That's something else we need to talk through because it sounds like your brother might have had something to do with that."

"What!" Ben looked angry. "My brother didn't have—"

"I'm sure he didn't mean to, but I think Marty might know more about that car accident than he's let on. You ask him and see if I'm right. But I'm not going to say anything to anyone about it, Ben. The fact is, what's done is done. And we *need* you. In fact, I don't think we can win without you. But win or lose, I think it's time we all got together and worked as a team. Think it over, Ben."

The two teammates looked at each other for a long time, then Chip turned and walked back toward the locker room. Ben Green stood in place, watching him go and thinking about what had been said.

CHAPTER 17

A Fighting Captain

MURPHY GILLEN had the floor. He and Diz Dean were arguing with Andre Durley and Ozzie Crowell. Chip heard their angry voices as he approached the locker room. He paused in the open doorway and surveyed the room.

Already in their blue and red State University uniforms and spikes, Speed, Soapy, and Red were standing together in one corner of the room. Other members of the team were in various stages of suiting up. The belligerent foursome, squaring off in the center of the room, held everyone's attention.

Doogie Dugan was sitting on the training table, and Murph Kelly was giving his pitching arm a rubdown. Terrell Sparks was standing beside the table waiting his turn. With the exceptions of Biggie, Fireball, and Burke, Ben Green was the only player absent.

"Is that so?" Gillen said angrily. "Well, let me tell you this! We had that game *won!* It wasn't because we didn't get any home runs. It was because Hilton and Green both lost their guts when the going got tough."

"Right!" Dean added. "And that's why we're out of the conference race."

Red Schwartz was first to spot Chip leaning against the doorway. He waved a newspaper in the air. "Chip!" he cried.

Dean and Gillen, their backs to Chip, whirled toward the door, their faces flushing scarlet. There was a general turning of heads, followed by an abrupt silence. Red advanced with the paper, but Chip brushed him aside and walked to the center of the room. "It looks like I arrived just in time," he said, facing Dean and Gillen.

"Since I'm here and you've already been talking about me, I've got a couple of things I want to get off *my* chest.

"First, let me say that I do feel responsible for the loss of the games last week. And you're absolutely right when you say I lost my guts, Gillen. I did. I was afraid to use my best pitch, my fastball. I take full responsibility for the loss of that game—and the others."

The room was tense. The players who were suiting up stopped right where they were, and Murph Kelly quit massaging Dugan's arm. The veteran trainer stared at Chip in shocked surprise.

"Now," Chip continued, "about Ben Green. All the things you have been saying about Ben are also my fault. I didn't do my part. If I had pulled myself together after the beanball trouble, we wouldn't have lost that game, and I don't think we would have lost any of the others either."

"That's a lot of nonsense!" a heavy voice said from the doorway. Ben Green stood there a moment and then walked swiftly to the center of the room and stopped beside Chip.

Chip was as surprised as the others. Apparently no one had seen or heard Green until he spoke. Chip faced Ben and started to speak, but the burly first baseman held up a hand. "Just a minute, Hilton. You had your turn. Now it's *my* turn."

There was something totally different about Green. The cocky, contemptuous grin was gone. Ben was now grim and deadly serious; even the bubble gum was gone. It was clear that the conversation he'd had with Chip outside had made an impression. Chip was amazed by the change in Ben's demeanor, and his teammates must have felt the same way. There was absolute quiet.

"Hilton," Green continued, "you did your part. Even when I was riding you and making a fool of myself, you were doing your part.

"I guess it will surprise you and the rest of the guys here, but I've been doing some deep thinking the last couple of days. You're a real gentleman and a real all-American, Hilton. I knew it all the time, but I wouldn't let myself admit it. You're also the only guy on the team who didn't get on me about losing the games.

"You didn't lose that Southwestern game. Man, my brother Marty could have caught that easy fly ball I muffed. I lost that game . . . and the others, but you never made any alibis. That shows you're more of a man than some of the gripers in this room who talk good games but never play any better than I do.

"I guess I might as well get everything off my chest, so here goes. Biggie Cohen is a great first baseman. I'm a novice compared to him. In fact, that junior college team I played for wasn't much better than a high school team. I don't belong on first base on the State University baseball team, and I know it. You guys would be undefeated right now if it weren't for me."

"Come off it, Ben," Chip said softly. "We—the team—lost the games. That's you and me and everyone else in this room. That's history. We're starting all over, as of right now! We've got a chance, and that's all a good team needs.

"I haven't declared myself so far in the argument about defensive baseball versus power baseball, but I'm going to do it. Right now! You elected me captain, and I'm going to show some leadership where it's needed. I'm joining Andre and Ozzie and playing their kind of baseball. They want to play as a team, and that's for me!

"The real ballplayers on this team are going to play team ball, and the rest of you can do as you please. I'm going to use every pitch I've got, including the fastball and the screw. I'll throw sliders and curves and every other one I know—with the exception of the beanball.

"I can still see Fox falling when my fastball hit him. I don't know how serious it turned out to be, but I do know my pitch wasn't intentional. Being able to throw my fast-breaking stuff again is something I've got to whip by myself, and I'm going to do it!"

"Wait a minute!" Red called, again waving the paper in the air. "This is something you ought to start with. Have you seen the evening *Herald*?"

Chip shook his head. "No, Red," he answered. "I haven't looked at a paper in over a week."

"You'll love this article!" Red said quickly. "It's about Bill Fox, the guy you beaned."

"He's all right, man!" Speed interjected. "He played last Saturday and was the big hero."

"That's right, Chip," Soapy added. "He hit for the cycle—got a single, a double, a three-bagger, *and* a home run! I was thinking maybe *I* ought to get hit in the head."

Chip looked quickly from Red to Speed to Soapy and then back to Red again. "You're kidding me," he managed.

"It's right here in the paper," Red said excitedly, pointing to an article on the sports page.

Chip's heart leaped. He felt as if someone had lifted a ton of bricks off his chest. He took a deep breath. It was the first time, it seemed, he had been able to really breathe for the past ten days.

He felt a sudden and complete release. It was as if he had been imprisoned deep in a cave and then been rescued just when all hope was lost. He wanted to leap in the air and shout at the top of his voice.

Soapy's words cut through his thoughts. "That oughta help!" the jubilant redhead cried.

"Help!" Chip exploded. "You'll never know! Let me see that paper." He snatched the sports page out of Red's hands.

SOUTHWESTERN STAR FULLY RECOVERED
Fox Hits Comeback Cycle

Bill Fox, Southwestern University baseball star, has fully recovered from a beanball pitch on May 16 against State University. Fox celebrated his return to the team by hitting the "cycle" in his four times at bat here last Saturday.

There was more, but Chip handed the newspaper back to Red and looked around at his teammates' smiling faces. "Yes!" he said. "What a break! What a terrific break!"

"You're entitled to a break," Ben Green said quietly, "and you can count on me playing your kind of baseball—if you think I can do you or the team any good."

"Count me in," Darrin Nickels added, meeting Chip's eyes. "I've been a fool."

"So have I," Al Engle growled. "I'm with you!"

"We're all with him," Dean called out. "Right, Gillen?"

Murphy Gillen nodded. "Of course. I've been the biggest fool of all."

"Well, then," Andre Durley cried, "what are we waiting for? Let's go out there and show the Rock he's got a fighting ball club."

The team didn't waste any time getting suited up. Chip moved as fast as the rest of them. He was fired up with a terrific drive. It was the first time all year the guys had been solidly together. Soapy, Speed, and Red waited for him before they headed out on the field together and took their laps.

Henry Rockwell put them through a stiff workout. Chip shagged flies for a while, batted wholeheartedly, and finally teamed up with Dugan in throwing to Soapy. If the coach noticed any change in his team's fervor, he failed to show it.

Just before he called it a day, however, he walked past Chip and gave him a significant wink. Chip figured Murph Kelly had told the coach about what had happened in the locker room.

At the end of practice, when Rockwell blasted his whistle and sent them around the field, Chip caught up with Green and trotted along beside him. "I'd like to talk to you after we finish our laps, Ben. Got time?"

Green was puffing, but he grinned and said, "Sure. All the time in the world. Slow down a little, will you?"

Chip slowed his strides, and when the rest of the team finished and headed for the locker room, he suggested another lap. Green was puffing more now, but he nodded and they kept right on going. When they came in this time, they were the only people left.

They walked to the dugout and pulled on their warm-up jackets. Green leaned back against the bat rack. "Well, Chip," he said, "what's on your mind?"

It was the first time Green had ever called him by his nickname, and it brought a fleeting smile to Chip's face. "You may not like what I'm going to say, but it has to be done."

"Shoot!" Green said, grinning.

"It's about Marty."

Green's eyes narrowed. "Marty? My brother Marty?"

Chip nodded. Then, without mentioning names, he told Green all about the car incident and brought in the group of boys who played ball near the parking lot each night. Then, as delicately as possible, he brought Marty into it, stating that he had information that indicated the boy knew something about the matter. Green listened carefully to everything Chip had to say without interrupting him.

"Marty would never lie to me," Green said. "Where can we meet you at eight o'clock tonight?"

"How about Grayson's?" Chip asked. "Use the side entrance on Tenth Street."

"We'll be there," Green said firmly.

Soapy was still in the locker room when Chip and Ben came in. He waited until they showered, and then the three of them left together. There was still a bit of tension, but Chip knew that Ben felt the same way he did. He tried to dissolve the feeling by talking about the Wednesday game at Eastern. "It's a key game," he said. "We've got to win it."

"We've got to win 'em all," Soapy growled.

"We'll beat them," the big first baseman said. "Well, I live down this way, so I'll head off. See you later, guys."

Chip and Soapy continued on, and Chip told his pal about his talk with Green. When he finished, Soapy was quiet for a time.

"Chip, you remember what I told you about Professor Gill's psychology analysis? About people being insecure and frustrated?"

"I sure do, Soapy. Dr. Gill sure hit a home run where Ben was concerned. He had a struggle between his conscious and subconscious thinking."

"What made him make such an about-face?"

"His subconscious, of course!" Chip quipped.

Soapy laughed. "Sure, Chip, but what was his subconscious thinking about?"

"Why don't you ask Professor Gill?" Chip teased.

"Aw, Chip, come off it. What *really* made him change?"

"I don't know the psychological reason, Soapy. In my opinion, Ben wanted to belong to the team in the worst way, just like you and me and everybody else, really. You know how important it is to belong. People need and want to be on 'the team' in everything: sports, business, the community, and anything else they are involved in.

"Ben tried to get on the team by the only means he knew, by bragging and misrepresenting facts. It caught up with him, just like it catches up with every person who lies, cheats, or tries to be something he isn't. When the team, and especially his so-called friends, turned on him and blamed him for losing the games, I think it just about broke his heart. But he learned a lesson from it and started looking at things with a different perspective when that happened.

"Underneath, Ben's a great person. He just didn't know how to go about being one of the guys. Now he knows."

CHAPTER 18

Just Another Batter

CHIEF MADERA flipped on the porch light and peered through the side window. Surprised, he opened the front door of his stone house and ushered his three visitors into the entrance hall. "Go right into the living room and sit down," he said, looking curiously at Marty. Chip sat down on one side of the long brocade sofa with Ben and Marty on the other. Chief Madera sat down directly opposite them in a wing chair.

"Well," Madera said, "I know all three of you fellows pretty well, so we can dispense with the preliminaries. It must be something pretty important to make you come here and not wait until the morning. What's on your mind, boys? Hilton, suppose you start off."

"I think Marty can tell it a little better," Chip answered.

Marty swallowed, peered uncertainly at Ben, and then started to talk. "I was playing ball on the field Sunday night with my friends, like we do lots of nights. We'd all seen Biggie Cohen drive the red car to the clinic that afternoon." Marty looked again at his brother before continuing.

"My group hadn't been invited to the baseball clinic, and we wanted to get even. The red car had one of the back doors unlocked. We got in and pretended to drive—we were just having fun, honest," Marty pleaded. "Nobody wanted to do anything really bad.

"Then somebody said it would be a good joke if we hid the car in the trees next to the parking lot. We were having fun, and I didn't think about it much. One boy got behind the steering wheel. He let off the brake, and the rest of us pushed the car out of the space. But the boy driving didn't put the brakes on quick enough, and then Biggie's car banged into the car parked in space number 20.

"We got scared then and didn't know what to do. Somebody said we should at least push the car back into its space, so we did. And we remembered to lock it too. Then we all ran home." Marty hung his head and leaned forward on the couch. "I know what we did is wrong, Chief Madera. I'm sorry."

"Who drove the car?" Chief Madera asked.

Marty leaned forward once more and peered at Ben. It was a pitiful plea for help, but Ben didn't respond this time. Instead, his jaw was firmly set and his lips were pressed tightly together.

"I . . . please, Chief Madera," Marty said, choking up, his eyes brimming with tears, "please don't make me tell. I'll do anything to make up for it. You're not going to arrest me, are you?"

Chief Madera studied Marty for a long minute. Finally he said, "No, Marty, I'm not going to arrest you. But you've got to be punished some way—you and the whole bunch.

"I've known Ben since he was your age, maybe even younger. Ben is a big, strong young man, and he's kept out of trouble even though he played around with some pretty tough kids. Unlike you, he had enough courage to walk away from anything that looked like trouble. He wasn't afraid of being called a chicken when the gang had a wild idea. Pranks can be fun, but they can also develop into something serious—especially when they concern other people's property.

"You're a big kid, too, Marty, just like your brother was. But you don't have Ben's strength of character, so I'm going to leave the punishment up to Ben. Personally, I think he ought to ground you and make you stay home every night and study, Monday through Friday."

"Don't worry about that, sir," Ben said grimly.

"As far as the rest of the kids are concerned," Madera continued, "I'm going to call them together and make them admit what they did. If they don't, I'll close the field and run them off the campus every time I see them."

He turned in his chair and reached for a pencil and pad of paper on the reading table. "Chip," he said, scribbling some notes on the paper, "I want to thank you for clearing up this mess. I'll see that Cohen is taken off the probation list first thing in the morning. That will automatically remove his name from the ex-athletics roll too."

"I'm afraid not," Chip said ruefully. "He missed too many classes—he's through for the year."

"I'm sorry to hear that," Madera said. He rose from his chair and led them to the door. "Young man," he said, grasping Marty's hand, "I hope you've learned a lesson."

"I'm through with those guys and with goin' out at night and—"

"With chewing bubble gum," Ben added, smiling.

That brought a little laugh from the chief, relieving some of the tension. The three visitors said good night and shook hands with Chief Madera. They walked down the sidewalk and turned toward town. Chip decided to walk home with them, and they continued on for some distance without a word. Then, obviously making an effort to be friendly, Ben began to talk about the upcoming game with Eastern.

When they reached the Greens' house, Marty thanked Chip and said he was going to bed. Ben said good night to the boy and watched him until he had entered the house and closed the door.

"Baseball isn't the only place where I struck out," Ben said sadly. "I didn't know Marty was running around with that bunch at night. He was always in bed when I got home. I guess a big brother has a lot of responsibilities that he doesn't give much thought to. Leading and guiding little brothers is a big job."

Ben paused. They were busy with their own thoughts for a time. Then he continued, "I'm just beginning to realize that, and I can thank you for making me wise up."

"I didn't do anything."

"Yes, you did. You know, it's hard for a kid to keep up with a gang of kids and stay out of trouble. Kids need friends, but sometimes it's hard for them to choose the right kind. Sometimes, when their parents live in a tough neighborhood like ours, the kids might think they don't have much choice. Then, if they get in with the wrong bunch, they almost have to go along with them in the things they do. That's when they need help, and that's where I failed. If there were more men like Coach Travis around, this town's kid trouble would be eliminated."

"I know," Chip said. "I met Coach Travis; he's a great man." He turned away, anxious to get back to his job, but Green stopped him.

"I feel pretty low tonight, Chip," Ben said haltingly. "Can you stick around a little longer?"

"Sure," Chip said understandingly. He was amazed how well everything had turned out. The team was back on track, and hopefully things with Ben would continue to improve. *Things turned out pretty well,* he thought gratefully.

"How about we sit on the porch?" Ben said. "You know, it took a lot of guts for you to confront me about Marty. Lots of guys would have figured it wasn't worth it and passed it up and just let the kid get into big trouble later."

Chip smiled slightly and shook his head. "I wouldn't have done it any other way. Biggie means a lot to me, and I wanted to get him off probation in the worst way, and I was pretty sure that you would want to know about Marty. As a Christian, I felt it was the right thing to do."

Chip looked directly at Ben and continued. "I've been thinking about you a lot these past weeks. The truth is important to me, Ben, and also I believe that we all have different purposes. This business with Biggie was tough, but it wasn't a coincidence. It gave me an opportunity to talk with you about some important things—like what your brother is doing and how we can all work together as a team."

"I've been a jerk, I guess," Ben admitted.

"Hey, nobody's perfect," Chip quickly responded.

Ben smiled and extended his hand. "Thanks again, Chip."

Chip shook the big athlete's hand and grinned. "No problem, Ben. Besides, I was just paying you back for what you taught me."

"What did I teach you?" Ben, surprised at the comment, searched Chip's face.

"You taught me never to play the other fellow's game. I'll never be a big hitter, a home-run specialist like you. And I'm never going to try it again. I'm just a pitcher. That is, I hope I still am. Anyway, it all depends on whether I can get my confidence back."

"You mean you feel that way too?" Green asked, astonishment ringing in his voice.

"Sure I do! I haven't been able to let a fastball really go since that beanball pitch."

"You'll do it," Green said firmly. "You're a real ballplayer. I don't think I'll ever be any good."

"With your ability? Nonsense! You're just out of position, that's all."

"Where else could I play?"

"You would be a fine catcher. You have an extremely strong arm, and you certainly know baseball. You could be a pitcher too. As far as hitting is concerned, as soon as you slow down your swing and stop trying to hit from your heels, you'll be a great hitter, and priceless as a pinch hitter."

"You're kidding. I couldn't be a catcher or a pitcher."

"Why not? I started out in high school as a catcher. Then I played first base. I never thought I would be a pitcher."

"I can't get any wood on the ball, Chip. I'm in a terrible slump, and I feel like a fool up there. I've tried everything. I wish I had your swing."

"I'll make a deal with you," Chip said lightly. "You help me get my confidence back, and I'll help you with your batting. All right?"

Green nodded. "Absolutely! When do we start?"

"Tomorrow after practice." Chip rose from the porch chair and extended his hand. "I need to get back to the store now. I'll see you tomorrow."

He finished out the evening at Grayson's and went to bed as soon as he reached Jeff. For the first time in a week he slept soundly. With Ben Green in line, Biggie's problem solved, and the Statesmen united as a team, everything seemed to have come together all at once. Now he could concentrate on his own problem.

There were still some "What happened?" questions on campus the next day, but they no longer irritated him. He was more concerned with the future than the past. Coach Rockwell put the team through a light workout that afternoon and called off practice early, but Chip, Soapy, Speed, Red, and Ben remained on the field. As they had discussed the previous night, Chip wanted to work against a hitter from the mound, and he wanted to help Ben with his hitting.

He warmed up from the game rubber with Soapy giving signs just as he would in a regular game. Ben was teeing off at the plate while Red and Speed chased the hits. Chip advised Ben to use a wider stance and a heavier bat, and the first baseman seemed to have improved his timing with these changes. Ben began to pull his bat through smoothly and soon was connecting with solid blows that sent the ball on slow-rising trajectories to the fences.

Toward the end of the special practice, Soapy called for his pal's fastball. Chip blazed it in. Ben was late with his swing, but he nodded happily when Chip's ball zipped past his bat. That was what Chip had been building up to all afternoon. He grunted with satisfaction. He could finally smoke his fastball in toward the hitter without holding back! Soon afterward, the guys called it a day, showered, and went home. They were ready for the next day's trip and to take on Eastern.

It was a perfect day for baseball. The sun was bright and warm, and there wasn't a cloud in the sky. Rockwell had called off the starting lineup in the locker room, but when Chip walked out to the mound to take his warm-up throws, he mentally checked on his teammates by their positions. Soapy was behind the plate, Green on first, Crowell at second, Durley on third, and Speed at shortstop. Red, Donovan, and Gillen were in the outfield, playing left, center, and right field, respectively.

Engle took Chip's warm-up throws. When Soapy walked out to the plate carrying his mask and glove, Chip threw the ball over to Durley. The little third baseman grinned his wide smile at Chip, and suddenly the pitcher lost his nervous emotion. Andre trotted over and handed the ball to him. The other players began their old, familiar chatter. Everything was all right!

The Eastern leadoff batter stepped up to the plate and dug in with his spikes. Right then Chip felt his chest tighten, and a little blood vessel in his throat started to throb a mile a minute. Standing behind the rubber, he waited for Soapy to squat and give the sign. He knew what the redhead was going to call. Soapy took his position and called for a fastball. Chip nodded and took a deep breath. It was now or never!

The plate looked a mile away, and Chip waited a moment to get rid of the illusion. He stepped forward, toed the rubber, took a full windup, and fired his fastball with desperate abandon toward Soapy's target. The redhead opened his glove wide, and the smack of the ball against leather reverberated back from the stands and down through Chip's body from his head to his toes. He had poured his fast one through, and the batter had stood as if paralyzed.

Soapy called for two more, and the Eastern leadoff man went down on three called strikes. That did it! He struck out the next batter and made the play to first himself when the third hitter bounced the ball weakly to the right of the mound. Three up and three down!

The Statesmen came in to bat and went to work on their planned routine as if it were a practice game. Crowell walked, and Morris went out at first on a bunt, but Ozzie advanced to second base. Schwartz lined to right field and Crowell scored. The pitcher cut off the throw to the plate and Red held up at second. Green hit a sharp grounder to the second baseman and was out at first, but Red broke for third and slid safely under the throw to the hot corner.

Chip, batting in the fifth spot, now came up to bat. He looked at a ball, took a called strike, watched another outside pitch go by, and cracked the two-and-one pitch to left center. Red scored and Chip held up at first base. Donovan cracked the first pitch and hit a long, high fly to the right fielder. The score at the end of the first inning: State 2, Eastern 0.

That was the story of the game. Chip overpowered the Eastern batters with his blazing fastball, darting curves, and change-up pitches, and the Statesmen methodically continued their carefully planned batting pattern. The final score: State 10, Eastern 0.

It had been a "must" win for the Statesmen, but it didn't improve their standings in the conference race. Northern University was still far ahead with a record of fourteen and three. Southwestern University was in second place with fourteen wins and four losses. State's standings were a dismal eleven and four.

Brandon University came to town on Friday for a weekend series. Dean and Sparks combined their pitching talent to win the first game 9-6. Chip duplicated his Eastern performance on Saturday in the second game to lead the Statesmen to a 5-0 victory. On Sunday morning Soapy came bustling in with the papers only to find that the Statesmen were still in third place, though making headway. The conference standings:

Northern	Won 15	Lost 3
Southwestern	Won 15	Lost 4
State	Won 13	Lost 4

State was hitting on all cylinders. When the Statesmen journeyed to A & M and Chip pitched them to their fourth victory in eight days, the fans began to sit up and take notice. The win over the Aggies brought the State record to fourteen victories and four defeats. Northern had split two games, and its lead had been cut to a single game over Southwestern and two games over State.

Chip, Soapy, Red, Speed, and Ben kept right on working at their special practice sessions. Ben was keeping his eye on the ball until it met his bat, and he began to tag the ball regularly with the extra practice. Chip devoted a little time every day to teaching Ben the rudiments of pitching, concentrating on showing his student straight power throws and the secrets of control he used. Green was like a kid with a new toy, and he loved every minute of it.

With the end of school in sight, a special kind of fever

began to grip the State campus. There were parties, dances, class reunions, graduation rehearsals, job interviews, and vacation plans. The sports calendar was jammed with golf and tennis matches, track meets, and baseball games. Most fans overlooked the Statesmen's closing rush for the conference title.

Southwestern came to town Friday morning for a two-game series. The visitors were in second place in the conference race with a record of fifteen wins and four losses.

That afternoon State combined eleven hits with superb defensive play to score a 9-8 triumph. Suddenly and deliriously, everyone realized that the State University Statesmen had overtaken Southwestern University and now occupied the runner-up position behind Northern, the league leader.

Alumni Field's grandstand and bleachers were packed with eager fans Saturday afternoon when Chip toed the rubber to start the second game of the series against Southwestern. He was worried about his reaction when Bill Fox made his first appearance at the plate, but after his first pitch to the SWU star, a fastball, Fox was just another batter. Chip struck the cycle hitter out twice, walked him once, and forced him to ground out in his fourth time at bat.

Chip's fastball was sailing and hopping, and he never let up, pouring it in and using it to the max. The Statesmen's attitude of taking the games one at a time was proving consistent and successful. They pecked away, inning after inning, and led by a score of 7-3 when the Southwesterners came up for their last at bats in the top of the ninth.

Chip and Soapy took care of all the outs in that last frame. Chip struck out the first batter, forced the second hitter to pop up to Soapy, and set the final batter down with three straight fastball pitches.

HOME RUN FEUD

That victory enabled the Statesmen to reach idle Northern University's record of sixteen victories and four losses. The two teams were tied for the conference lead! The championship game on Wednesday at Alumni Field would end the season for both teams and produce the Division 1 champions.

CHAPTER 19

Dust in His Eyes

"HERE THEY COME!" Mark shouted. As if released out of the blocks by a starter's gun, the home-run kids, with Mark Parsons and Marty Green leading the pack, raced toward them. Chip, Soapy, Speed, Red, Biggie, Fireball, and Ben barely had time to look at one another and smile before they were mobbed. The little guys grabbed their arms, patted them on the backs, crowded against them, shrieked questions, and then answered them all in the same breath.

"You gotta win today, Chip!"

"Ben, you better hit home runs!"

"Yeah, Ben, it's our last chance for baseballs until next year."

"Speed, you better be fast today!"

"Hey! Soapy! Are you catching?"

"We'll be pulling for you guys!"

"Stand 'em on their heads, Chip."

"Fog 'em past them like you did against Southwestern."

Chip caught a glimpse of Ben's face and smiled happily. Chip could tell that the big player had never enjoyed so much popularity with kids in his life. Two months ago all of the kids except for Marty and the tough crowd he was hanging around with would have avoided Ben. But not anymore.

Kids were hard to fool, and this bunch knew baseball. They had read the papers and understood that the Statesmen had made it to where they were because they had forgotten all about personal glory and instead played together as a team.

They had reached the players' gate now, and the kids were giving them a last bit of advice, patting them on their backs just once more, hanging on for the last word, searching for one more glance of recognition, a wink, or a smile. The players passed through the gate and still the kids stood there, pushing one another, craning their necks, waving and hollering, "Good luck!" and "You can do it!" and "We're with you!"

On the way into the locker room, Chip pulled his arm up to make a muscle, released it, and pushed down as hard as he could. No matter what he did, his arm still felt like a stick of wood. He had noticed it Sunday morning before church services but hadn't given it much thought. On Monday it was throbbing, and when he tried to warm up, a streak of pain shot from his elbow to his shoulder.

He had managed to evade Murph Kelly on Monday, but yesterday the veteran trainer had found him during practice and examined his arm. It didn't take Kelly long to find out there was something wrong.

Chip dressed slowly. Kelly had been resolute, and Coach Rockwell had backed him up. There would be no pitching for him in this game, championship or no championship. An hour later, Chip was in the dugout eating his heart out, sitting the bench, knowing there was not a thing he could do about it.

He was still sitting there when the Statesmen ran out on the field to start the game. He checked the lineup. Engle was behind the plate, and Diz Dean was on the mound. Green,

Crowell, Durley, and Speed made up the infield, and Schwartz, Donovan, and Gillen were in the outfield. He shook his head dubiously, knowing this wasn't the powerful ball club that had won the national championship a year ago. Not that it couldn't have been just as powerful. He glanced sideways at Biggie, Fireball, and Belter Burke. Coach had let them sit in the dugout, and Chip wondered what they were thinking. One thing was sure. It would be a long time before they forgot this game, especially if State lost.

The Statesmen *had* to win today! If they won, their school would benefit and they would gain national attention. Biggie, Fireball, and Belter might even be eligible to play in the NCAA championship tournament if they passed all their courses.

If only he hadn't thrown so many fastballs against Southwestern! He could only hope his arm would be all right in a week. If they won today, he hoped to pitch in the national tournament.

It was a tight, hard-fought battle, a tense struggle for every run and every out. Dean was wild, as usual, but the Statesmen were battling for their very lives and making one sensational play after another. Thankfully, the Northerners weren't having a field day at the plate. Dean was just wild enough to keep them wondering where the next pitch might go.

Northern loaded the bases in the top of the fourth, and Rockwell had to call on Sparks. Before Flash could put out the fire, Northern had scored two runs. The Statesmen got them back in the bottom of the sixth.

When Northern came to bat in the top of the seventh, Sparks walked the first two hitters. Coach Rockwell immediately called time. It was a tough spot. After a short talk with Engle and Sparks, Rockwell called Doogie Dugan in to replace Sparks. Fortunately, the third batter grounded to Speed, and he and Crowell executed their specialty, doubling up runners at first and second. The lead runner was held at third. Two away! The next Northern batter slashed a hard drive to left field. Schwartz pulled it in on the dead run for the third out.

The game went into the last inning with the score still tied at two all. Then Dugan got the shakes. He walked the first batter and hit the second, and once more Rockwell called time and lumbered out to the mound for a conference. *Now what?* Chip said to himself. He knew Dugan was through. Chip could see it in the little pitcher's face. Without pausing to think, he walked quickly out to the diamond and joined the huddle.

"Try Ben, Coach," he urged earnestly.

"Ben! He's never pitched, Chip."

"He has a lot of speed and good control. He can do it, Coach. I've been working with him. Give him a try."

"All right," Rockwell said dubiously. "Let's give it a whirl."

Ben was scared to death. He started to back away, but it was too late. Coach Rockwell sent Darrin Nickels in to replace Ben at first base. Ben had no alternative but to walk up to the mound. He took his warm-up pitches with Chip standing there giving him all the support he could.

"Control, Ben," Chip urged. "Throw hard and keep the ball in the strike zone. Just throw like we practiced."

Ben nodded and took a deep breath. "I'm scared," he breathed. "Scared to death."

The umpire called, "Play ball!" Chip went back to the dugout, offering a silent prayer for Ben. He turned to watch as his friend toed the rubber and threw the ball to the plate. There was a sharp crack before the ball shot high in the air and headed deep into center field.

Donovan turned and took off, looking over his shoulder at the ball all the while. He was nearly under the ball when the man on second tagged up. The runner on first had gone with the hit and was nearly to second base when Donovan suddenly tripped and fell clumsily to the ground! The ball hit the bottom of the fence.

All the runners kept moving! The ball rebounded from the fence and sped past Crowell, who had gone out as a relay man. The ball kept coming on the ground, hard and fast and straight to Speed.

What happened next showed why baseball is such a great game.

Speed grabbed the ball and threw a perfect strike to Engle, who tagged the lead runner as he slid home. Green had backed up the play at home. "Third base, Engle! Third base!" he yelled.

Engle fired the ball to Durley. The hot-corner guardian tagged the incoming runner for the second out. The batter had made a wide turn at first base and, thinking Donovan might make the catch, had held up. When Donovan tripped, the batter dug his spikes in and tried to make it down to second, but Durley threw a clothesline peg to Crowell. The second baseman put the ball on the runner for the third out. It was an unbelievable triple play—made the hard way!

The State fans went wild. Chip was exhausted and as limp as a wet rag. He was finding the incredible play hard to take in. The Statesmen came charging in now. They were still in this ball game because of the triple play, one that only Speed and Andre and Ozzie could have executed. It was their kind of baseball.

Murphy Gillen got his bat out of the rack, but Rockwell suddenly bounded out of the dugout and stopped him. "Chip!" he called, "hit for Gillen."

Chip was caught completely by surprise. He grabbed his favorite bat and the warm-up stick and loosened up. Despite the gravity of the situation, he was thinking that a player never knew what the Rock would do next. He walked up to the righty side of the plate and got set.

The first pitch was in there, and he tagged it. The ball landed over third base and hugged the foul line clear to the fence. He made it to second base and pulled up with the roar of the crowd booming toward him. Rockwell called time again and then sent Soapy in for Donovan.

Soapy took a long time getting to the batter's box. Chip knew what the redhead was thinking: Any kind of a hit would bring him in and win the game.

No one could hear a thing now. The fans were stomping their feet on the bleachers and yelling and cheering and pleading for a hit until the clamor sounded like one continuous roar of thunder.

Soapy never even had a chance to hit. The very first pitch hooked in and caught him in the shoulder. He walked slowly down to first base.

Green was up now. Chip took a good lead. He was carrying the winning run, and he wasn't going to get doubled up at third base. Ben went through his ritual. Chip watched eagerly, wanting to remind the first baseman not to forget what they had been practicing but hesitant to break Ben's concentration. "Just meet it, Ben!" he yelled. "Smooth and easy."

The first pitch was outside. The next was a little high, but Ben went for it and hit a hard grounder to the second baseman. Chip was off toward third. The Northern second baseman saw that he had no chance to get Chip at third base and threw the ball to the shortstop, who cut the ball across first base for the double play.

Then, for the first time, the Northerners realized that Chip had kept right on going. He had turned third base at top speed and was now racing for the plate. The first baseman was caught by surprise, although he recovered quickly and his throw to home plate was perfect. But Chip got there first, sliding across the plate a split second before the catcher tagged him.

Looking up through the cloud of dust, Chip saw the umpire's arms shoot out to his sides, and he knew he was safe. The Statesmen had come from nowhere to win the conference championship!

Chip didn't know who reached him first. He only knew that Ben and Soapy and Fireball and Biggie and Speed and Red and Engle and Durley and Crowell and the home-run kids quickly had him on their shoulders. And then he saw the Rock. Chip's coach was holding his fists up in the air and shaking them and grinning at Chip with that crooked grin that always assured Chip that all was right with the world.

Alumni Field had erupted into pandemonium as fans scrambled all over the field. "We did it!" Chip exulted. He reached for his teammates' hands and cheered as loudly as the rest. He found Ben Green's big hand and clasped it tightly.

"You did it! You pitched, Ben." Chip smiled broadly at his new friend, proud of what they accomplished together.

"Thankfully, it was only one pitch," Ben said, beaming proudly and laughing at the same time. "I'll leave next week's pitching to you."

"We're going all the way!" Soapy called out, throwing his hat in the air. "There's nothing to stop *this* team from taking the title again!"

At that moment, there was no place Chip wanted to be more. He smiled proudly at his friends and cheered right along with them, thrilled to be part of the winning team.

• • •

It's summer time, and Chip answers an urgent call from the Valley Falls mayor. A full-scale crisis is brewing and Chip Hilton holds the solution and must return.

Be sure to read *Hungry Hurler,* an action-packed baseball book and the next exciting story in Coach Clair Bee's Chip Hilton Sports Series!

Afterword

THE CHIP HILTON SPORTS SERIES has helped me a lot. First, it helped me to give all I've got when I'm playing basketball, baseball, soccer, or whatever I'm doing, and to have good sportsmanship. The books also helped me to be strong in any troubles I might have. Chip and his friends did these things and have shown me a good example to follow.

Second, Chip always wanted to help others no matter what the cost was. In *Ten Seconds to Play!* (#12), Chip suffered a black eye, a cut lip, and more to get Philip Whittemore out of a jam. In *Fourth Down Showdown* (#13), Chip misses a few games because of curfew to help Isaiah and Mark Redding. In *Hardcourt Upset* (#15), Chip and his friends lose a lot of sleep helping clear Soapy Smith's name of a chain of gas station robberies.

Third, it has helped me to do something else in the summer besides watching TV or going to the pool. I have always enjoyed reading books, but I never liked them enough to re-read them annually every summer and each time enjoy them as much as the last. Thank you, Chip, Coach Bee, and Mr. and Mrs. Farley for giving me such a good example to follow.

Joshua Neuhart
Student—Brownsburg, Indiana

THE CHIP HILTON SPORT SERIES BOOKS, written by Coach Clair Bee, have been inspiring our family for more than thirty-five years. As a young boy in the 1960s, I discovered one of Coach Clair Bee's books in the school library in Belmont, Ohio. I was enthralled with the characters of Chip Hilton and his friends—Taps Browning, Speed Morris, Soapy Smith, and Biggie Cohen—and their coach, Henry "The Rock" Rockwell.

I remember reading that first book, entitled *Hoop Crazy*, over and over again. Chip and his friends were teammates on the Valley Falls High School basketball team. Being the defending state champion, the Valley Falls Big Red team was expected to successfully defend their state title and had started off the season by winning their first five games. Hopes were high; excitement in the town was mounting with each victory, and suddenly it happened. Everything started to go wrong. The team was losing. There was a stranger in town, who offered hope with a new style of shooting the basketball and playing the game. Would he be the savior for the Valley Falls team? Would Coach Rockwell lose his job? Would Chip discover what was causing the problem that was destroying the team? I wouldn't spoil the mystery for you. You'll have to get the book and find out for yourself.

As the coach of a fifth and sixth grade basketball team at Bethesda Christian School in Brownsburg, Indiana, and a father of three children, I wholeheartedly recommend the Chip Hilton Sports series books. Coach Clair Bee was a brilliant coach and innovator. He wrote stories that were realistic and exciting. He used his stories to teach the fundamentals, strategies, and history of basketball, football, and baseball. He taught me about the importance of practicing the fundamental skills, helping your teammates develop their potential, persevering in the face of obstacles, and taking a stand to do what is right in spite of peer pressure. I became a better player and person because of what I learned from Coach Clair Bee's stories.

AFTERWORD

It is thrilling to see my son, Joshua, and his friends reading and enjoying the Chip Hilton series. They play on their school soccer, basketball, and baseball teams. Like Chip and his buddies, Joshua and his friends—Travis Penner, Caleb Adkins, Josh Silver, Jake Haeffner, Doug McGinnis, Josh Black, J. D. Thomas, Scott Poytner, and Chris Phillips—have experienced the sorrows and joys of losing and winning championship games. More importantly, they are learning the lessons from Chip Hilton about perseverance, hard work, dedication to excellence, and teamwork.

To Coach Bee's daughter and son-in-law, Cindy and Randy Farley, I thank you for updating and republishing the Chip Hilton books. Our family and countless others have been inspired and blessed by your dad's books.

John Neuhart
Coach, Pastor, and Dad

Your Score Card

I have I expect
read: to read:

———   ———   1. ***Touchdown Pass:*** The first story in the series introduces readers to William "Chip" Hilton and all his friends at Valley Falls High during an exciting football season.

———   ———   2. ***Championship Ball:*** With a broken ankle and an unquenchable spirit, Chip wins the state basketball championship and an even greater victory over himself.

———   ———   3. ***Strike Three!:*** In the hour of his team's greatest need, Chip Hilton takes to the mound and puts the Big Reds in line for all-state honors.

———   ———   4. ***Clutch Hitter!:*** Chip's summer job at Mansfield Steel Company gives him a chance to play baseball on the famous Steelers team where he uses his head as well as his war club.

———   ———   5. ***A Pass and a Prayer:*** Chip's last football season is a real challenge as conditions for the Big Reds deteriorate. Somehow he must keep them together for their coach.

———   ———   6. ***Hoop Crazy:*** When three-point fever spreads to the Valley Falls basketball varsity, Chip Hilton has to do something, and fast!

HOME RUN FEUD

I have   I expect
read: to read:

_____   _____   14. ***Tournament Crisis:*** Chip Hilton and Jimmy Chung wage a fierce contest for a starting assignment on State University's varsity basketball team. Then adversity strikes, forcing Jimmy to leave State. Can Chip use his knowledge of Chinese culture and filial piety to help the Chung family, Jimmy, and the team?

_____   _____   15. ***Hardcourt Upset:*** Mystery and hot basketball action team up to make *Hardcourt Upset* a must-read! Can Chip help solve the rash of convenience store burglaries that threatens the reputation of one of the Hilton A. C.? Play along with Chip and his teammates as they demonstrate valor on and off the court and help their rivals earn an NCAA bid.

_____   _____   16. ***Pay-Off Pitch:*** Can Chip Hilton and his sophomore friends, now on the varsity baseball team, duplicate their success from the previous year as State's great freshman team, the "Fence Busters"? When cliques endanger the team's success, rumors surface about a player violating NCAA rules—could it be Chip? How will Coach Rockwell get to the bottom of this crisis? *Pay-Off Pitch* becomes a heroic story of baseball and courage that Chip Hilton fans will long remember.

_____   _____   17. ***No-Hitter:*** The State University baseball team's trip to South Korea and Japan on an NCAA goodwill sports tour is filled with excitement and adventure. East meets West as Chip Hilton and Tamio Saito, competing international athletes, form a friendship based on their desire to be outstanding pitchers. *No-Hitter* is loaded with baseball strategy and drama, and you will find Chip's adventures in colorful, fascinating Asia as riveting as he and his teammates did.

HOME RUN FEUD

About
the Author

CLAIR BEE, who coached football, baseball, and basketball at the collegiate level, is considered one of the greatest basketball coaches of all time—both collegiate and professional. His winning percentage, 82.6, ranks first overall among major college coaches, past or present. His name lives on forever in numerous halls of fame. The Coach Clair Bee and Chip Hilton awards are presented annually at the Basketball Hall of Fame, honoring NCAA Division 1 college coaches and players for their commitment to education, personal character, and service to others on and off the court. Coach Clair Bee is the author of the twenty-four-volume, best-selling Chip Hilton Sports series, which has influenced many sports and literary notables, including best-selling author John Grisham.

Chip Hilton Sports Series

CHIP HILTON MAKES A COMEBACK!

The never-before-released *VOLUME 24* in the best-selling Chip Hilton series will be available soon!

Broadman & Holman Publishers has re-released the popular Chip Hilton Sports series that first began in 1948, and, over an ensuing twenty-year period, captivated the hearts and minds of young boys across the nation. The original 23-volume series sold more than 2 million copies and is credited by many for starting them on a lifelong love of sports. Sadly, the 24th volume was never released, and millions of fans were left wondering what became of their hero Chip Hilton, the sports-loving boy.

Now, the never-before-released 24th volume in the series, titled *Fiery Fullback*, will be released in Fall 2002! See www.chiphilton.com for more details.

START COLLECTING YOUR COMPLETE CHIP HILTON SERIES TODAY!

1224

Bee, Coach Clair

Home Run Feud

Chip Hilton Sports Series # 22